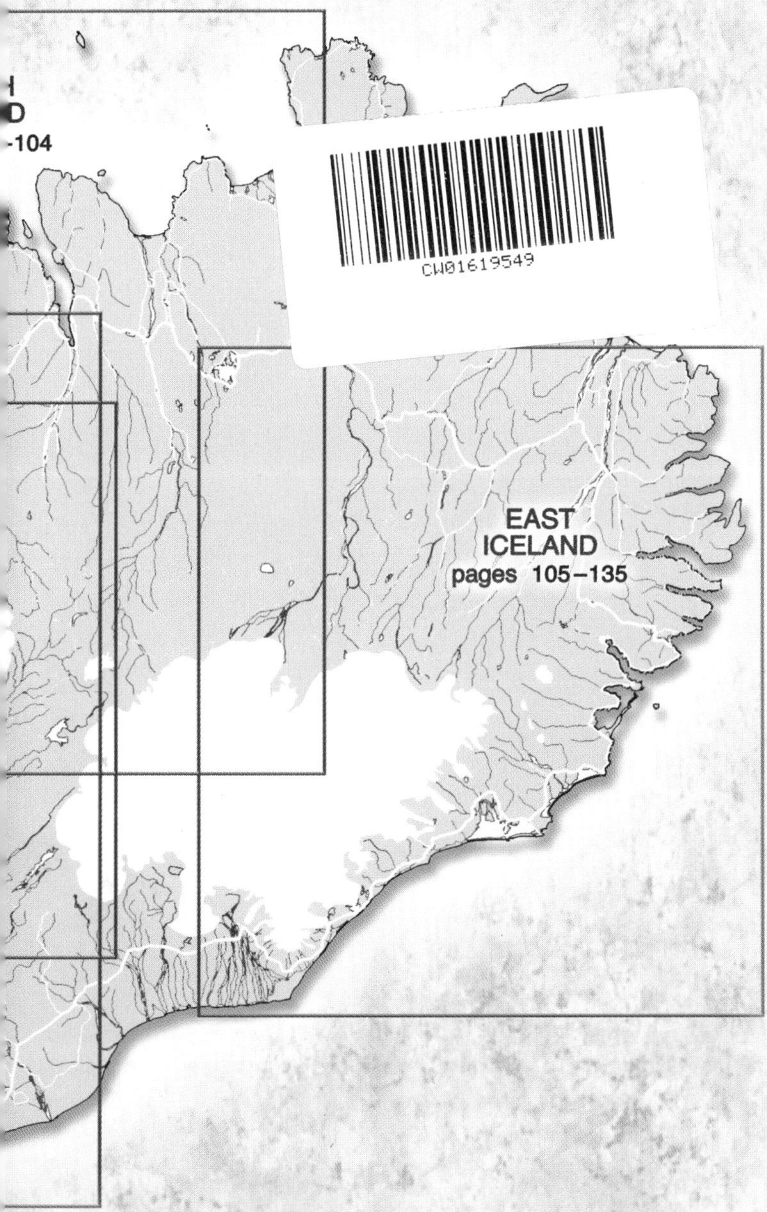
EAST
ICELAND
pages 105–135

A Traveller's Guide to Icelandic Folk Tales

Jón R. Hjálmarsson

A Traveller's Guide to Icelandic Folk Tales

Translated by Anna Yates

Iceland Review

A Traveller's Guide to Icelandic Folk Tales

Originally published in 2000 by Almenna bókafélagið under the title *Þjóðsögur við þjóðveginn*.
This edition published by Iceland Review ©, an imprint of Edda Media & Publishing Ltd, Reykjavík, Iceland, 2002.

Verses translated by Bernard Scudder

Cover design: Loftur Leifur Ólafsson/Auglýsingastofa Skaparans
Maps: Ólafur Valsson
Illustrations: Ólafur Pétursson, SKÓP
Design: Magnús Valur Pálsson

Printed in Iceland

ISBN 9979-51-190-7

Contents

NORTH ICELAND

EAST ICELAND

SOUTH ICELAND

HIGHLANDS

Categories of Folk Tales

Tales of elves, votive offerings and various sacred and enchanted sites.

Tales of ghosts, spectres and other strange creatures, and their relations with humans.

Tales of resourceful wizards and their remarkable skills.

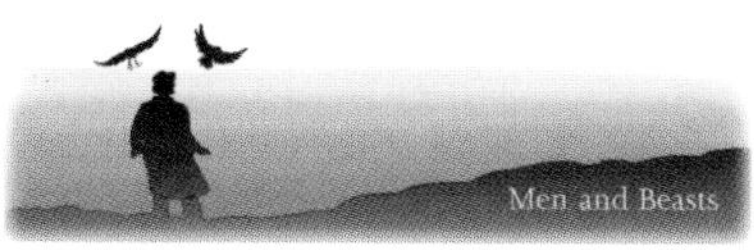

Tales of men and beasts, strange events and great feats.

Tales from mythology and the nether world, mostly concerned with the Devil's dealings with men.

Tales of trolls and other monstrous creatures.

Foreword

In this book we take a tour around Iceland, along the Ring Road and side-roads all over the country – in imagination at least. We also make a few excursions into the central highlands via little-used mountain tracks. Along the way we pause at popular tourist destinations, as well as other places which are less well known, to recall the folk tales and legends associated with them.

The scene is set for each story with a description of the surrounding landscape and a brief history of the area, as well as practical information about routes to the various locations. We travel through the west, the West Fjords, the north, the east, the south and finally the central highlands.

The tales tell of a wide variety of mysterious phenomena, including men with magical talents, "hidden people" or elves, ghosts, trolls, monsters, beasts and even the Devil himself, to name but a few. All the stories are based on existing folk tales but some have been slightly adapted and shortened in line with the format of the book, without altering the essentials of the tale.

Folk tales are an important part of any nation's cultural heritage. Iceland has a great and varied store of such tales, which give their own picture of the ideas and beliefs of past generations. Some stories contain familiar motifs that also occur in the folklore of other countries – and indeed supernatural experiences are no respecters of national boundaries.

I sincerely hope that readers will enjoy the tales in this book, whether they carry it with them on their travels around Iceland – or simply take an armchair tour through the nation's folklore.

Jón R. Hjálmarsson

A Note on Icelandic Pronunciation

The letter þ (capital Þ) is pronounced like the "th" in English "thing", and the letter ð (capital Ð) like the "th" in "then".

WEST ICELAND

1. Redhead, the Evil Whale of Hvalfjörður

Hvalfjörður is one of the more spectacular regions through which one passes on the way from Reykjavík to the north or west of Iceland on the Ring Road. Today a tunnel (opened in 1998) leads under its mouth, but it is worth taking the detour around this long and picturesque fjord, especially in fine summer weather. Hvalfjörður (Whale Fjord) cuts into the land from Faxaflói bay, between Akranes and Kjalarnes. It is about 30 km long, 4–5 km across and 80 m deep at its deepest. In the outer reaches of the fjord there is some lowland, but towards the head of the fjord steep cliffs rise straight from the sea. At its inland end the fjord forks into two branches, Brynjudalsvogur and Botnsvogur. Hvalfjörður is surrounded by splendid mountains, such as Þyrill and Reynivallaháls in the south, and Múlafjall, Hvalfell (Whale Hill) and Botnssúlur at the head. To the east of Hvalfell is a large lake, Hvalvatn (Whale Lake), which is about 160 m deep. The river Botnsá flows from this lake and cascades down in the Glymur falls, by far Iceland's highest waterfall at 198 m. The origins of the place-names Hvalfjörður, Hvalfell and Hvalvatn (Whale Fjord, Hill and Lake) are explained in an old folk tale:

Once upon a time some men from Suðurnes, on the Reykjanes peninsula, went out to Geirfuglasker (Great Auk Skerry) to catch great auks. When it was time to return to land, one of the men was missing. So the rest of the group returned home without him, and the man was believed to have died. A year later, however, the same men returned to the skerry and found the man, safe and sound. It transpired that elves had placed a spell on him and kept him with them, treating him well. But he was not happy with the elves, and went ashore with the other men. By now, however, an elf woman was carrying his child and she made him promise to have the child baptised if she brought it to him at church.

Some time later, the man was at mass at Hvalsnes church. A cradle was found outside the church, with a note which read: "The man who is father of this child will make sure that it is baptised." People were astonished, and the pastor suspected that the man who had spent a year on the skerry was probably the father. He pressed the man to acknowledge that he had fathered the child but the man denied it. At that moment a woman appeared, tall and robust. She turned to the man and said: "I cast a spell on you, that you shall become the worst of evil whales in the sea and wreck many ships." Then she seized the cradle and vanished without trace, but people assumed that she must have been the elf woman from Great Auk Skerry, where the man had stayed.

After this the man went mad and took to his heels. He ran to the sea and jumped off the cliff named Hólmsberg, between Keflavík and Leira, where he was instantly transformed into the worst of evil whales; and he was called Redhead, for he had a red cap on his head when he flung himself into the sea. This whale proved a great scourge, and in the end he was said to have sunk nineteen ships between Seltjarnarnes and Akranes. Thus many people were harmed by him. As time passed, he began to take refuge in the fjord between Kjalarnes and Akranes, and so it came to be known as Hvalfjörður (Whale Fjord).

At that time there was a pastor at Saurbær, on the shore of Hvalfjörður, who was both old and blind. He had two sons and one daughter, who were fully grown and very promising. This pastor had supernatural skills. His sons often went out fishing on the fjord. One day they met with Redhead and he drowned them both. The pastor felt the loss of his sons deeply, and one day soon after this he asked his daughter to take him down to the fjord, which was not far from the farm of Saurbær. He took a stick and made his way down to the shore with his daughter's help. Then he stuck his stick into the ground at the tideline and leant forward onto it. He asked his daughter what the sea looked like; she replied that it was mirror-smooth and calm. A little later the pastor asked his daughter again what the sea looked like. Then the girl replied that she could see a black stripe coming up the fjord, like a big shoal of fish. When she told him that the stripe had reached them, the pastor asked her to lead him inland along the shore, and she did so. The stripe kept pace with them, to the head of the fjord.

But as the fjord grew shallower, the girl saw that the stripe was the wake of a huge whale, which was swimming straight up the fjord as if he were being led, or driven. At the end of the fjord, at the mouth of the Botnsá river, the pastor asked his daughter to lead him up the western bank of the river. She did so and the old man clambered up the mountainside, while the whale struggled up the river next to them, with great difficulty, since the river was small and the whale big. When the whale reached the gully where the river cascades down off the heath, there was so little space for him that everything shook as he struggled on. Finally, as he climbed the waterfall, everything around trembled as in the greatest earthquake and the rock made a thunderous roar. This is the origin of the waterfall's name, Glymur (Roaring), and the hills above the waterfall are known as Skjálfandahæðir (Shaking Hills).

But the pastor went resolutely on, and did not stop until he had brought the whale to the lake from which the Botnsá river flows, which has been called Hvalvatn (Whale Lake) ever since. A hill that stands by the lake also derives its name, Hvalfell (Whale Hill), from this event. When Redhead reached the lake, he expired from the strain of climbing there. Nobody has seen him since, but impressive whale bones have been found at the lake and this is deemed to prove that the tale is true. When the pastor had brought the whale up to the lake, he made his way home with his daughter and everybody thanked him for what he had done.

2. Tragedy at Barnafoss

In the upper reaches of the Borgarfjörður valleys, the Hvítá (White River) falls from the uplands, dividing the communities of Hvítársíða and Hálsasveit. The landscape of this region is varied and attractive; lowlands are interspersed with rolling hills, rugged lava fields and fragrant birch woods beneath the peaks of Strútur, Hafrafell, Ok, and the Eiríksjökull and Langjökull ice-caps. The farm of Kalmanstunga lies closest to the highlands on the northern side of the river, while Húsafell is closest on the southern side. There are various caves under the lava fields nearby, including Víðgelmir, Stefánshellir and Surtshellir, which was used as a refuge by outlaws long ago. Surtshellir, about 1,500 m long, is believed to be Iceland's largest lava cave; it is easily accessible, only about 7 km from Kalmanstunga.

Húsafell is an old church site. The best-known pastor of Húsafell was probably Snorri Björnsson, who served the parish from 1757 to 1803. A man of prodigious physical strength, the Rev. Snorri would demonstrate his prowess by lifting a rock, Kvíahella, which can still be seen at Húsafell; it weighs 180 kg. He would also challenge visitors to try lifting the rock. The Rev. Snorri was reputed to have magical powers, and he is said to have exorcised more than 80 ghosts which were sent to plague him. The place where the ghosts were laid is known as Draugarétt (Ghosts' Enclosure). The original parish of Húsafell was abolished in 1812 but a new chapel was consecrated there in 1973, based on designs by the artist Ásgrímur Jónsson (1876–1958), who often painted at Húsafell.

Extensive birch woods flourish at Húsafell and it is a popular spot for outdoor gatherings. Many summer houses have been built in the area, which has abundant geothermal resources to heat houses and a swimming pool. Various services for visitors, including a shop, are available there. Within the estate of Húsafell is the former farmstead of Reyðarfell, which was abandoned in the 15th century, and has recently been excavated. From Húsafell a mountain road leads south via Kaldidalur (between Ok and Langjökull) to Þingvellir (see p. 210).

The farm nearest Húsafell is Hraunsás. Adjacent to this farm, a little downstream from where the Norðlingafljót flows into it, the Hvítá river boasts some extraordinary waterfalls. The Hraunfossar (Lava Falls), about a kilometre in length, are a multitude of tiny, crystal-clear streams that flow from the edge of the lava field on the north bank of the river, cascading between rock, moss and birch into the murky waters of the glacial river.

Just upstream is Barnafoss (Children's Falls), where the Hvítá river swirls though a narrow gorge in spectacular falls and rapids. These falls are now traversed by a footbridge, but traces of old stone bridges can be seen in the gorge. According to folklore, the river was once bridged by a natural stone arch:

Once upon a time a wealthy woman lived at Hraunsás, and she had two young sons. One day she went with her entire household to church at Gilsbakki, north of the river, but both boys stayed behind. She told her sons to stay at home and not to stray from the house while she was away. But when everybody had gone, the boys grew bored and eventually they decided to go after the others to church. They walked down to the Hvítá river and soon reached the stone arch. The arch is said to have been rather narrow, with a long drop down to the river and the waterfall beneath. The boys were frightened and they held hands to cross the river. Things went well until they reached the middle of the stone arch and looked down into the maelstrom below. They grew so dizzy looking down into the eddies that they fell from the bridge into the river and drowned.

When the churchgoers returned home, the lads were nowhere to be found. Their mother ordered a search, but for a long time this was fruitless. Eventually she learned what had happened, for someone had seen the boys on their way to the river but had been too late to save them. The woman then grew very upset and angry, and she had the stone arch over the river broken down, saying that no one should cross it alive ever again. The waterfall has been identified with this event ever since, and is now known as Barnafoss (Children's Falls).

The mother was especially distressed that her sons' bodies were not found, so that they might lie in consecrated ground. She promised that she would give the estate of Norður-Reykir to the church in the parish where their bodies were washed ashore, and that she would give the estates of Hraunsás and Húsafell to the church where they were buried. Shortly after this, the boys' bodies were washed ashore near Norður-Reykir, in the parish of Reykholt. Her sons were laid to rest at Reykholt and all three estates passed into the possession of Reykholt Church.

3. Kolbeinn and the Devil at Þúfubjarg

The Ring Road continues northward, crossing the Borgarfjörður bridge. Shortly beyond the town of Borgarnes, the road to Ólafsvík branches off to the left and soon passes Borg á Mýrum, settled in the ninth century by Skalla-Grímur, and later the home of his son Egill, the warrior-poet and hero of Egil's Saga. The route through the Mýrar district runs across lowlands, while mountains such as Kolbeinsstaðafjall and Fagraskógarfjall rise to the right. The road then passes through the Hnappadalur valley, where the Eldborg volcanic crater lies to the left. To the right is Gerðuberg, a picturesque formation of columnar basalt. Nearby are the church site of Rauðamelur and Rauðukúlur, a cluster of unusual cinder craters. The mountain landscape is constantly changing. Soon the peak of Skyrtunna (Curd Barrel) comes into view on the right.

The road running west along the south coast of the Snæfellsnes peninsula is one of Iceland's most spectacular routes. Below the rhyolite peak of Mælifell, east of Axlarhyrna, there is a crossroads. To the right is the road onto Fróðárheiði, which leads to the east of the Snæfellsjökull glacier and down to the village of Ólafsvík; to the left is the turn-off for Búðir, a delightful spot that was once a trading centre. The road straight ahead leads onward around the end of the peninsula, passing Öxl, where the infamous Axlar-Björn (Björn of Öxl) robbed and murdered travellers in the 16th century, and on to Breiðavík. West of this is the fishing village of Arnarstapi, or simply Stapi, below Stapafell. The shore at Arnarstapi abounds in bizarre formations of columnar basalt, caves and fissures. A little farther west is the famed Gatklettur, where the sea has eroded a hole through the cliff. Arnarstapi is a popular tourist destination, offering accommodation, a campsite and a restaurant.

A little farther west is Hellnar, a hamlet by the sea. Here too, strange rock formations may be seen on the shore, including a cave known as Baðstofan (the baðstofa was the communal living/sleeping room in a traditional turf farmhouse). Above the village is Laugabrekka, the birthplace of Guðríður Þorbjarnardóttir, who with her husband Þorfinnur karlsefni attempted to settle in Vínland (North America) in the early 11th century. Their son, Snorri Þorfinnsson, who was born in America, went on to become a prosperous farmer at Glaumbær in north Iceland.

The Snæfellsjökull glacier dominates this area, reaching a height of 1,446 m, and the region is known as Undir jökli (Under the Glacier). The slopes and lowlands around the glacier are largely formed of lava, with little vegetation, but the landscape has a mystical beauty. Slightly west of the abandoned farm of Dagverðará is Malarrif, with a lighthouse at the outermost point. On the shore east of Malarrif are the Lóndrangar, rock pillars rising out of the sea, the tallest 75 m high. In times past, egg-gatherers used to climb the pillars in search of seabirds' eggs.

East of Lóndrangar is a small headland called Svalþúfa. Grass grows in the upper reaches, while a vertical cliff called Þúfubjarg rises from the shore, where the pounding of the waves has eroded caves and hollows in the cliff face. Bird life is abundant here, and the roaring of the sea mixes with the chattering of the birds in a natural symphony. From here it is just a short walk to Svalþúfa, which is a good spot for appreciating the natural wonders east of Malarrif – and for recounting the folktale of Kolbeinn, known as the "glacier-poet", and the Devil, who sat together on the cliff edge one night, exchanging verses, as the story goes:

Once upon a time, it is said that the Devil made a wager with Kolbeinn the glacier-poet. They were both to sit on Þúfubjarg cliff under the glacier, when the surf was at its wildest, and exchange verses. For the first part of the night the Devil should compose the first two lines, and Kolbeinn should complete the verses, while during the second part of the night the arrangement was to be reversed. And they resolved that he who could not complete a verse begun by the other should jump off the cliff and be from that day forth at the mercy of the other. And so they sat out on the cliff one night when the moon was shrouded in cloud. They exchanged verses all through the first half of the night: the Devil composed the first two lines and Kolbeinn completed the verses at once, with no delay. Then in the second half of the night Kolbeinn started composing the first two lines, and for a long time the Devil was successful in completing the verses. When the night was growing old, Kolbeinn saw that this could not go on. He took a knife from his pocket, and held it up to the Devil's eyes, so that the edge seemed to touch the moon, and said:

Look upon this blade blade
let the moon oblige oblige

Now the Devil was speechless, for he could not find a word to rhyme with "oblige". He became quite uncomfortable and said: "That's not proper poetry, Kolbeinn." At which Kolbeinn completed the verse himself, saying:

you whom I have made made
fall when I replied replied you.

When the devil heard this, he was so taken aback that he fell off the cliff and down into the wave that broke below. It is unlikely that Kolbeinn had any more trouble with the Devil after this, and certainly he was never again challenged by him to exchange verses.

4. Dritvík and Djúpalónssandur

The Snæfellsnes peninsula has been endowed with extraordinary natural beauty and variety. But rising above all is its crowning glory, the mysterious and mystical Snæfellsjökull ice-cap, 1,446 m high and about 11km^2 in area. Today many people make their way to the peak of the majestic glacier, following in the footsteps of the pioneers, Eggert Ólafsson and Bjarni Pálsson, who first scaled the ice-cap in the summer of 1754.

Interesting places in the south of the peninsula include Djúpalónssandur, a rounded, cliff-lined bay with two freshwater lagoons, a short distance east of the abandoned farm of Einarslón. Strange rock formations on the shore include Gatklettur, where there is a natural window in the rock, and Draugahellir (Ghost Cave), which was once thought to be haunted. Below Gatklettur lie three rocks that were used in the past to test the strength of prospective crewmen on fishing boats: Fullsterkur (Strongman) weighs 155 kg, Hálfsterkur (Half-strong) 140 kg, and Hálfdrættingur (Half-weight) 49 kg. There was a fourth rock, *Amlóði* (*Weakling*), which weighed 23 kg, but this is now broken. Djúpalónssandur was an important seasonal fishing station in past centuries.

Just north of Djúpalónssandur is Dritvík (Dirt Creek), a deep hollow between the edges of the lava fields. The southern section of Dritvík is called *Víkurbarði* or *Suðurbarði*, while the outermost part is known as *Vesturbarði*. Two rocks, Bárðarskip (Bárður's Ship) and Bárðartrúss (Bárður's Burden), are named after Bárður Snæfellsás, a semi-legendary saga hero. At the outer part of the bay is Dritvíkurbjarg (Dritvík Cliff); between this and Bárðarskip is a narrow strait, which is hazardous to vessels but leads to a good landing-place. Dritvík was an important seasonal fishing centre until the 19th century, as it was close to rich fishing grounds. At that time, 60 to 70 boats rowed from Dritvík, crewed by 300 to 400 men. Many fishermen's shelters and fish-drying enclosures could once be seen at Dritvík, although little now remains of them. Dritvík had the disadvantage of lacking fresh water, which had to be fetched from Djúpalónssandur along a path named Vatnsstígur (Water Path). At the outermost point of the peninsula at Dritvík there are cliffs in which there is a cave called Tröllakirkja (Trolls' Church).

Dritvík and Djúpalónssandur are beautiful and interesting places, where the environment is highly unusual and history is found at every step. It is worth making a detour from the main road, as it is a mere 3 km to the shore.

There are many folktales and traditions connected with this stretch of the coast, including the following:

The story goes that some of the fishermen rowing from Djúpalónssandur were such brave seamen that they feared nothing. They tested their strength by lifting rocks. These rocks still lie at Djúpalónssandur, slightly above the road. Their names are "Strongman", "Half-strong" and "Half-weight"; nobody was permitted to row from Djúpalónssandur unless he could lift "Strongman" on to a plinth at waist height. These strong fishermen of Djúpalónssandur are said to have seized an old woman and killed her. Others say that they took her body from the bier, while some claim that they dug up her newly buried corpse. They used her body for bait one spring, and their catches were so large that they had to stack their fish for drying every day, although the other crews hardly caught anything. They all used the woman's flesh for bait, except one half-weight who rowed with them, named Sigurður. One night he dreamed that a woman came to him and shouted aloud:

Tomorrow a ship will be breached,
a wondrous event will be reached;
do not go forth tomorrow morn,
Sigurður, of a wonder I warn.

Others claim, or add, that she said: "Thou shalt not row this day: now I shall make a stir beneath my bones." In the morning Sigurður pretended to be ill, but the rest rowed out and all of them drowned that day.

There is a cave a short way west of Dritvík. It is said that a little while later some men were travelling near the cave when they heard a noise there, as if someone was speaking. It is said that one or two men on the ship were from Helgafell, and that one of them was friendly with the daughter of the farmer of Hólahólar, named Narfi. Those who approached heard this verse chanted in the cave in a deep voice:

Lying in this dank cave is dull;
life is better in Helgafell,
with dancing and wrestling withal.

Then another spoke, so clearly that they heard and understood:

In the fishes' realm I venture deep,
far into the water;
though numb, I still can homeward creep
to Narfi from Hólar's daughter.

The mouth of the cave faces downwards. It is said to be true that some of the bodies were washed up there in stormy seas, and it has been known as Draugahellir (Ghost Cave) ever since.

5. Sacred Hill of Three Wishes

A tour around the Snæfellsnes peninsula is an unforgettable experience for anyone with an interest in impressive landscape, varied bird life, and the mysterious Snæfellsjökull glacier. But the glacier is not the only place to which folk tradition attributes supernatural qualities; another such place is Helgafell (Sacred Hill) in Helgafellssveit. This is a low hill on the northern side of the peninsula, which stands to the right of the road leading to Stykkishólmur. This picturesque formation, rounded to the west and south, edged with cliffs to the north and east, is only 73 m high, yet it rises majestically from the lowlands. Supernatural powers are attributed to the hill: tradition says that anyone who climbs it according to certain rules may make three wishes, which will be fulfilled, provided they are benevolent ones.

To the south of Helgafell is a farm of the same name, which is famous in Icelandic history. It stands on the bank of Helgafellsvatn (Helgafell Lake). Helgafell was originally settled by Þorsteinn the Cod-biter, son of Þórólfur Örnólfsson, who had settled at Hofsstaðir in Helgafellssveit. The assemblies held on his estate, at Þórsnes, were among the precursors of the Althing, the general assembly at Þingvellir founded around AD 930, which is said to be one of the world's oldest parliaments.

One of the sons of Þorsteinn of Helgafell was Þorgrímur, who was slain by Gísli Súrsson, as recounted in the Saga of Gísli. *Gísli was outlawed and ultimately killed for this offence. Another of Þorsteinn's sons was Börkur the Stout of Helgafell, one of Gísli's most implacable enemies. Gísli's sister Þórdís was married first to Þorgrímur and then* to Börkur, which complicated the issue. Þórdís was famous for inflicting a severe wound on Eyjólfur the Grey, who had killed Gísli, in revenge for her brother's death. This led to the divorce of Börkur and Þórdís, after which Börkur left Helgafell. The estate was then taken over by his nephew, Snorri Þorgrímsson, who soon became an influential chieftain, regarded as wise and gifted with foresight, but also rather cold and vengeful. Among other things, Snorri played an important role at the time of Iceland's adoption of the Christian religion in AD 1000. He converted to Christianity and had the first church built at Helgafell. A church has stood there ever since.

In his old age Snorri exchanged homes with Guðrún Ósvífursdóttir, who lived at Sælingsdalstunga in the Dalir region. Guðrún, one of the protagonists of Laxdæla Saga, has a rather ambiguous reputation, but in her old age she lived a virtuous Christian life. She was buried at Helgafell and her grave is believed to be north of the nave of the church, above the churchyard. A memorial was placed there many years ago, with Guðrún's name and the date 1008, which was believed to be the year of her death. In 1184 a monastery was built at Helgafell. The monks moved there from Flatey island, where there had been a monastery for about a decade. With the foundation of the monastery, Helgafell developed into a centre of religion and culture, where many important and beautifully illuminated manuscripts were produced over the centuries. This continued until the Reformation in the 16th century, when the Helgafell monastery was dissolved and robbed. Many of its books were burned on a bonfire, as was common at that time. The Lutheran cleric who had the books burned did not survive for long; he drowned in the lake a year after the blaze.

Many remarkable clergymen have served at Helgafell: one of them was Sæmundur Magnússon Hólm, who served in the 18th and into the 19th century. He was eccentric, and constantly in dispute with his neighbours, but also an excellent poet and artist; he had been a prize-winning student at the Academy of Art in Copenhagen. Many of his portraits survive.

West Iceland

SNÆFELLSNES

From early times, supernatural powers were attributed to Helgafell by those who lived nearby. They regarded it as a sacred place and named it Helgafell (Sacred Hill). The settler Þórólfur believed so strongly in the sanctity of the place that he ordered that no one might look towards the hill without washing. The hill was also a place of sanctuary, where no person or animal might be killed. Þórólfur and his sons believed that they would be taken into the mountain when they died.

The settlers were heathens who worshipped the Norse gods Þór (Thor) and Óðinn (Odin) and others, yet belief in the sanctity of the hill persisted even after the conversion to Christianity. After the monastery was founded at Helgafell, the monks made a little chapel on the hill. Traces still remain of a stone foundation, which is said to be the remnants of the monks' chapel.

There has also been widespread belief in the tradition of the three wishes that are granted to those who climb Helgafell. According to the experts on such matters, the method is something like this: set off from the grave of Guðrún Ósvífursdóttir and walk up the hill. Do not look back or speak a single word on the way. When you reach the top, stop at the chapel ruins, look to the east and silently make three wishes. If these instructions are followed precisely, it is said to be highly likely that the wishes will come true, but only of they are made with goodwill, are harmful to no one and are not repeated to anyone. Many people are said to have tried this over the centuries, with good results. Travellers in the north of the Snæfellsnes peninsula may wish to bear this in mind.

6. The Elf Church of Tungustapi

*History and natural beauty combine with unusual power in the Dalir region of west Iceland. Just a short journey northward along the main road from Búðardalur, the main community of Dalir, is Sælingsdalur (Sælingur's Valley), which leads to the northwest from Hvammsfjörður. Through this verdant, picturesque valley meanders the Sælingsdalsá river. One of the estates in the valley, Sælingsdalstunga (*tunga *= a tongue of land), features in* Laxdæla Saga*: it was the home of Guðrún Ósvífursdóttir and her husband Bolli Þorleiksson. After Bolli slew his old friend and rival Kjartan Ólafsson, Guðrún exchanged homes with Snorri of Helgafell, who moved to Sælingsdalstunga. In Sælingsdalstunga Snorri built a church of which one can still see some traces. Adjacent to the farm of Sælingsdalstunga, commonly called simply Tunga, is Tungustapi, an impressive rocky outcrop above the Sælingsá river. This has long been reputed to be the home of elves or "hidden people". It was said to be an elf cathedral and episcopal see. A folk tale says:*

Many centuries ago a wealthy farmer lived at Sælingsdalstunga. His children included two sons, Arnór and Sveinn, both fine men, though in different ways. Arnór was gregarious and often amused himself with other youngsters. They would often meet up at the rock by the river known as Tungustapi. In the winter they slid on the hard snow down off the rock, with shouting and merriment. Sveinn rarely took part in this; he generally went to church while the others were at play. He was also solitary and often went to the rock alone. It was the general opinion that he mixed with the elves; on every New Year's Eve he disappeared and no one knew where he went. Sveinn often asked his brother not to make so much noise by the rock, but Arnór mocked him and said he had no sympathy for the elves just because of a little noise.

One New Year's Eve Sveinn vanished as usual. People started to wonder what had become of him and Arnór volunteered to go looking for him. He walked off in overcast weather to the rock. Suddenly, the rock opened up on the side that faced the farm, revealing innumerable lights within. He heard the most wonderful singing and he realised that the elves were celebrating Mass. Approaching, he looked through the door and saw the church filled with people. A priest in splendid vestments stood at the altar and there were many rows of lights on both sides. He walked into the church doorway and saw his brother, Sveinn, kneeling at the altar, while a priest laid a hand on his head. Arnór concluded that he was being ordained and called out loudly: "Sveinn, come, for your life is at stake." Sveinn was startled and made as if to go to his brother. At that moment, the man at the altar called out:

"Lock the church doors, and punish the human who has disturbed our peace. But you, Sveinn, must leave us, and that is your brother's doing. And because you placed more value on his call than on your ordination to the priesthood, you shall fall down dead the next time you see me here in these vestments." The men in their canonicals lifted Arnór, and Sveinn saw him vanish up into the stone vault over the church. At that moment, bells began to ring loudly and all those within rushed to the doors. Arnór ran home as fast as he could, hearing elves riding behind him with a clattering of hooves. He heard one of the leading riders chant:

Ride, ride, dark is the mountainside,
cavort, transport the wretch away,
never more to behold the light of day,
the light of tomorrow's day.

The riders swept by, between Arnór and the farmhouse, and he had to retreat. On the slope below the farm the elves rode over him and he was left lying more dead than alive.

Sveinn arrived home late at night. He was withdrawn and did not speak much, but he felt that a search must be made for Arnór. They searched for him all night, until finally the farmer of Laugar, on his way to matins, came across him on the slope, very weak. He told the farmer all that had happened that night, but he was too weak to be moved and he expired in that place, which has been known since then as Banabrekka (Death Slope). After these events, Sveinn was never the same again, growing ever more grave and melancholy. He soon abandoned all worldly things and became a monk at the Helgafell monastery. He was the most learned of men and sang Mass more beautifully than anyone else.

When Sveinn's father grew old, he fell gravely ill. And when he felt that he had only a short time left to live, he sent for Sveinn to come from Helgafell. Sveinn did as he was asked but said that he might not return alive. He arrived at Tunga on the Saturday before Easter, to find his father close to death. Sveinn's father asked him to celebrate Mass on Easter Sunday and gave orders that he should be carried into church, so that he might die there. Sveinn was reluctant but agreed, on condition that the church doors should not be opened during the Mass, as his life was at stake. This was regarded as a strange request but people concluded that he did not wish to see the rock: in those days the church stood on a low hill in the homefield and the church doors faced the rock.

The farmer was carried into the church and Sveinn donned his vestments and began to sing Mass. Those who were present said they had never heard such sweet singing or such excellent intoning, and they were as struck dumb. But when the pastor turned from the altar and began to pronounce the Blessing, suddenly a westerly gale struck, blowing open the church doors. The congregation were startled and turned to look. They saw what appeared to be an open doorway into the rock, from which shone innumerable lights. And when the congregation turned back towards the pastor, he had collapsed and expired. At the same moment, his father too had fallen from the pew and was also dead. The weather was calm both before and after this event, so it was clear to all that the storm from the rock was not a natural occurrence.

Among those who witnessed these events was the farmer of Laugar, he who had found Arnór at the point of death many years before, and he recounted the whole story. Then they understood that what the elf bishop had said to Sveinn – that he would fall down dead the next time he saw him – had come to pass. When the rock stood open and the church doors flew open, the doors faced each other, so Sveinn and the elf bishop saw each other – for the doors of elf churches face in the opposite direction to human ones. After this event, a regional meeting was held and a decision was made to move the church from the hillock down into a hollow closer to the farmhouse. This meant that the farmhouse stood between the rock and the church doors. Never again has the pastor been able to see through the church doorway to Álfastapi (Elf Rock) – and no such extraordinary events have happened since.

10 Hornstrandir
Ísafjarðardjúp
9
Bolungarvík
Ísafjörður
11
Dranga-
jökull
Arnarfjörður
Hrafnseyri
Bíldudalur
8
Patreksfjörður
7
Látrabjarg
Brjánslækur
Hólmavík
Steingríms-
fjörður
12
Breiðafjörður

WEST FJORDS

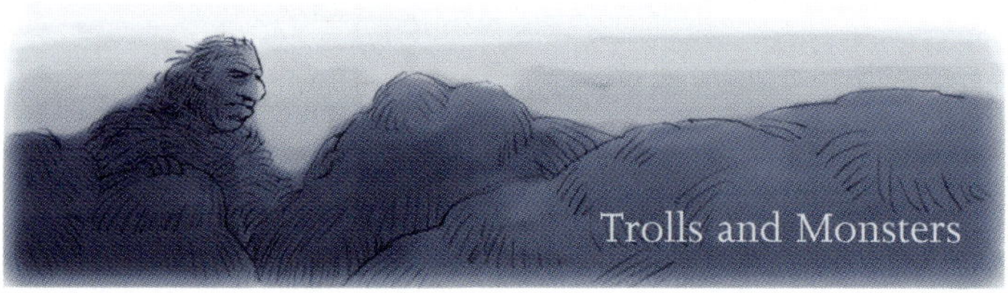

7. The Monster of Látrabjarg

The route following the indented coast of Barðastrandarsýsla along the southern part of the West Fjords leads to the beautiful fjord of Vatnsfjörður. This is where Flóki Vilgerðarson, known as Raven-Flóki, made an attempt to settle Iceland in the 9th century, some decades before the settlement began in earnest; it was he who gave Iceland its chilly name. He is commemorated by a monument there, and the restaurant by the river Penna is named Flókalundur (Flóki's Grove) in his honour. From Vatnsfjörður, a route leads over Kleifaheiði to Patreksfjörður. At the head of the fjord, the road forks: one route leads to the village of Patreksfjörður on the northern side of the fjord, while the other route, to the south, passes through Sauðlauksdalur and into a lovely valley called Örlygshöfn (Örlygur's Harbour). There is an interesting folk museum there, at Hnjótur. Continuing out of Örlygshöfn, the route crosses Látraheiði, leading to Látrabjarg.

Látrabjarg (Látrar Cliffs), at the westernmost point of the north coast of Breiðafjörður, are among Iceland's most impressive sea cliffs. The cliffs end at Bjargtangar, the westernmost point of Iceland, and indeed of Europe. North of Bjargtanger is Látravík, and the farm of Hvallátur, the most westerly habitation in Iceland. There were once many households here, gaining a living from farming and the fisheries, as well as by trapping seabirds and gathering their eggs. Látravík was a busy fishing centre in past centuries and remnants of old structures from that period can still be seen. There are also rocks here, which men used to lift to test to their strength. One of them, named Brynjólfssteinn (Brynjólfur's Rock), weighs 350 kg. A man named

Brynjólfur carried it from the shoreline up onto the crest of the beach – he was no weakling.

Látrabjarg is 14 km long. All the cliffs are quite high and most of them perpendicular. At their highest point, at Heiðnakinn, they rise 444 m above the sea. Several small valleys cut into the cliffs: Djúpidalur in the west, then Geldingaskorardalur, and in the east Lambahlíðardalur. Many of the gullies and rocky belts are rich in vegetation, and in the past they were even used for haymaking. Here and there, projections of harder rock, which the sea has not eroded, stand out from the cliff; one of these, Barð, is about 60 m high. Many ships have sunk off Látrabjarg and many seamen's lives have been lost there. The last vessel to run aground at Látrabjarg was the British trawler Dhoon, just before Christmas of 1947. All the trawler's crew members were rescued by local people, despite perilous conditions. But seamen were not the only ones at risk at Látrabjarg – those who climbed down the cliffs to collect eggs and trap birds were also in danger. The cliffs often yielded tens of thousands of birds in a summer and even more eggs, a valuable and prized resource. But traditional bird trapping and egg gathering on the cliffs has not been practised since 1925: the following year, two young men fell to their deaths, and after this the custom ceased. There are many tales and traditions about Látrabjarg, including the following:

In the days of Bishop Guðmundur Arason the Good [13th century], it transpired that men were sure that a monster resided in Látrabjarg and was spoiling the fishermen's catch. Also, at that time, those who climbed down the cliff for birds and eggs had so many accidents that it was deemed suspicious. It often happened that, when a climber was down on the cliff, those who were waiting above in charge of the rope suddenly saw that the man was gone – and later he was found, dead and mutilated, at the foot of the cliff. When the end of the rope was examined, it would appear to have been severed with a sharp blade. At that time, a man named Gottskálk lived at Hvallátur. He was a skilled man and was said to have mysterious powers, yet he had no effect upon this rock-dweller, although he is believed to have tried. Then Gottskálk and the others who used the resources of the cliffs took this problem to Bishop Guðmundur the Good. The bishop saw that action must be taken, so he went west to the cliff and summoned the rock-dweller to appear. The bishop upbraided him harshly for his persecution of the men, and said he would drive him off the cliff. The rock-dweller begged for mercy and asked to be allowed to stay, saying, "A black sheep must have somewhere to go." Then the bishop's ire was mollified and he asked the monster how much land he needed. The rock-dweller then said that the bishop could decide that himself, when he knew how big his family was. The bishop asked how many there were and the rock-dweller replied: "I have twelve ships off the shore; on each ship are twelve men, each man has twelve harpoons, and for each harpoon there are twelve seals. Then I cut each seal into twelve pieces, and there will be one piece for each of us and also two for each seal's head: so you count, sir."

And so the bishop gave the rock-dweller permission to live with his family in the part of the cliff that has since been called Heiðnabjarg (Heathens' Cliff). This was the part, stretching from Djúpidalur to Saxagjá, where it was most difficult for humans to trap birds and gather eggs. The bishop forbade the creature to go beyond these boundaries, and then he began to consecrate the cliffs. He consecrated all but Heathens' Cliff, and he forbade all Christian men to climb there or to utilise the cliff in any way. At this, the persecution by the rock-dweller ceased and he was never seen again – and the bishop's ban on gathering eggs and trapping birds on Heathens' Cliff was not broken for many centuries.

8. Sorcery in the West Fjords

The southern region of the West Fjords boasts spectacular scenery. There is little lowland, the mountains are high and the fjords many. This is an interesting region for the traveller, constantly offering new and fascinating prospects. There are two routes into the West Fjords from the north coast of Breiðafjörður: via Vatnsfjörður, across Dynjandisheiði and into Arnarfjörður, or over Kleifaheiði to Patreksfjörður. This latter route leads to the thriving village that bears the same name as the fjord, Patreksfjörður, then continues into Tálknafjörður, where another pleasant fishing village has grown up. From Tálknafjörður, a mountain road named Hálfdan leads to Bíldudalur in Arnarfjörður, yet another attractive little fishing settlement.

Arnarfjörður is the largest of the West Fjords south of Ísafjarðardjúp, about 30 km in length, and 5–10 km across, stretching from Kópanes in the south to Sléttunes in the north. The inland end of the fjord forks into two. South of the Langanes peninsula are Suðurfirðir (the South Fjords), the northernmost of which is Geirþjófsfjörður, which features in the Saga of Gísli. North of Langanes is Borgarfjörður, from which Dynjandisvogur bay extends. The landscape is attractive, with wooded slopes and, not least, the splendid waterfall Dynjandi or Fjallfoss, where the river Dynjandi tumbles off the edge of the plateau down a series of rock strata, spreading out into a picturesque, multi-layered cascade 100 m high.

Arnarfjörður boasts many historic sites, such as Selárdalur, the outermost of the Ketildalir dales, a church site. One of the most famous pastors of this parish was Páll Björnsson, who served in the 17th century, a period of witch hunting in Iceland. An excellent scholar and prosperous landowner, the Rev. Páll grew so obsessed with witchcraft that he had many people burnt at the stake for supposed offences. At the farm of Selárdalur there is a rock into which three hollows have been carved. It is attributed to Árum Kári – according to folklore, a pastor at Selárdalur. Brautarholt in Selárdalur was the home of self-taught artist Samúel Jónsson, and many of his sculptures and buildings may still be seen there.

In the north of Arnarfjörður is Hrafnseyri, another church site. In the Saga Age this was the home of Hrafn Sveinbjarnarson, who is said to have been Iceland's first qualified physician. His neighbour, Þorvaldur of Vatnsfjörður, so envied Hrafn's success that he eventually had him killed in 1213. At Hrafnseyri there are ruins of a church believed to date from the 12th–13th century; this is a listed building. Hrafnseyri became well known once more in the 19th century, as the birthplace of Jón Sigurðsson (1811–79), leader of Iceland's independence movement. He is commemorated by a monument and museum at Hrafnseyri. The church at Hrafnseyri, which dates from 1886, contains various items of interest, including old church bells. From Hrafnseyri, the West Fjords route continues over Hrafnseyrarheiði to Dýrafjörður, over Gemlufjallsheiði to Önundarfjörður, and finally over Breiðadalsheiði and via a tunnel to Ísafjörður.

Arnarfjörður is not only known for its natural beauty and history; the region also has long been notorious for various kinds of sorcery and witchcraft. A master of these arts in the 19th century was Jóhannes Ólafsson of Kirkjuból in Mosdalur, a valley that extends from the north of the Langanes peninsula, parallel with Hokinsdalur. There are many tales of his supernatural powers, which were said to be so great that a mere greeting from him would exorcise ghosts. The story is told of a woman in Bitrufjörður, who was persecuted by a family ghost until she was on the brink of madness. She sent a man to Jóhannes to ask for his aid. He responded helpfully, writing some runes on a piece of paper and asking the messenger to take them to the woman. She was to fling the piece of paper at the ghost the next time she saw it and tell it that Jóhannes of Kirkjuból sent his greetings. The woman did as instructed, rid herself of the ghost and soon regained the best of health.

Just inland from Bíldudalur is Otradalur, formerly a church site. During the Saga Age this was the home of Eyjólfur the Grey, who slew Gísli Súrsson at Einhamar in Geirþjófsfjörður, according to the *Saga of Gísli*. In the 18th century, the parish of Otradalur was served by the Rev. Bernharður Guðmundsson, a skilled versifier who was reputed to have supernatural knowledge. He was involved in a dispute with a Tálknafjörður man named Ármann who lived at Eysteinseyri. Ármann had some grudge against the pastor and so he wakened up a ghost known as Klaufi (Hoof), for his cloven hooves. But the pastor was so skilled in magical arts that he succeeded in defending himself and his wife against this visitor, although Klaufi killed some of his livestock. The pastor was most unhappy with the way that this scourge followed him around, killing off bulls belonging to farmers where he was making pastoral visits. The pastor did his best to exorcise the ghost but without success. He then consulted another Tálknafjörður man, named Grámann, who was known to have powers of witchcraft, and asked him to put Klaufi to rest. Grámann said this would be a difficult task but he was prepared to try. But the ghost was so powerful that the earth would not accept him, except at one hillock in the land of Lambeyri, where Grámann finally succeeded in laying the ghost. This place was so poisonous that no animal or bird could touch it without falling down dead. And not a blade of grass has grown there since.

9. Þjóðólfur and Þuríður the Strait-filler

Bolungarvík is a thriving fishing town in the outer reaches of Ísafjarðardjúp, on the western shore. The community received its town charter in 1974 and the population is now more than 1,200. The bay (Icelandic: vík), from which the name of the town is derived, faces northeast and stretches from Óshyrna in the south to Traðarhyrna in the north. To the west of Bolungarvík is Stigahlíð, where steep slopes and cliffs make the terrain hard to traverse. Two grassy valleys lead back from the bay, with Mt. Ernir above. At the mouth of these valleys stands the estate and church site of Hóll, formerly an important manor. The landscape of Bolungarvík is spectacular, with abundant vegetation in some areas, and there is an impressive view across Ísafjarðardjúp to Grænahlíð, Jökulfirðir, Vébjarnarnúpur and Snæfjallaströnd.

Bolungarvík is believed to have been a seasonal fishing centre from the earliest days of Iceland's history, thanks to its proximity to rich fishing grounds. In times past, fishermen's huts stood there in clusters, but permanent habitation did not develop for a long time. It was only after Bolungarvík became a trading post in 1890 that people began to settle there permanently. The hamlet was licensed as a trading centre in 1903, and in 1911 harbour construction commenced. The local economy has been largely based on the fishing and fish-processing industries, although there have also been other enterprises. While today's fisheries employ state-of-the-art technology, Bolungarvík also offers the opportunity to learn about the old ways: a replica of an old fishing station has been built at Ósvör, showing how fishermen lived *and worked in the days of the rowing boat. Reconstructions of a fishermen's shelter, fish-drying shack and salting shack have been built, along with other items connected with fishing in the past. At nearby Gil in Syðridalur, where lignite (brown coal) was mined for fuel in 1917–21, traces can be seen of old mine-workings.*

In the past, Bolungarvík was isolated and difficult to reach except by sea. The community became more accessible when the Hnífsdalur-Ísafjörður road via Óshlíð was opened in 1950. This road, however, is a hazardous one, due to the risk of falling rock and avalanches from the slopes above, and it is constantly being repaired and improved. Another road leads from Bolungarvík via Skálavíkurheiði to Skálavík, a community which is now only inhabited in summer. Skálavík has a long and interesting geological history: some of Iceland's oldest rock strata have been found there, dating back 15–16 million years.

L*andnámabók* (the Book of Settlements) tells of Þuríður *sundafyllir* and Völu-Steinn, her son, who came from northern Norway and settled at Bolungarvík. Þuríður had remarkable powers, and it is said that before she left Norway, during a time of famine, she cast a spell that filled all the straits with fish, hence her sobriquet *sundafyllir* (Strait-filler). The following folk tale tells of her relations with her brother Þjóðólfur.

The Hólsá river rises in the Tungudalur valley in Bolungarvík and flows a short distance before reaching the sea in the middle of the bay. At the top of the bay, north of the river, is a farm with fine buildings, which some say was named Þjóðólfstunga. For Þuríður the Strait-filler had a brother named Þjóðólfur. He asked Þuríður to give him a piece of land at Bolungarvík, and she allowed him as much land as he could fence in a day. He set off and built a wall from Stigi, intending to fence off Hlíðardalur and Tungudalur, but got no farther than the middle of Tungudalur that day. Traces of the wall can still be seen. Þjóðólfur laid claim to both valleys, but Þuríður claimed she owned the valley that was not fully fenced off, and she expected him to submit. Þjóðólfur was very displeased and wished to avenge himself by stealing an ox that Þuríður kept at Stigahlíð. She noticed him there and chased after him, but he took the beast and tried to lead it home.

They met at Ófæra. She immediately fell upon him and tried to take the beast away, but without success. Now she was so angry that she cast a spell upon him, that he should be turned into a rock in a place where multitudes of birds would leave their droppings. He retorted that she should become a rock in the place where the strongest winds blew – and since then she has stood at the top of the northern point of Óshlíð, as may clearly be seen. As for Þjóðólfur, he turned to stone and fell down into the sea, where he landed on a rock that stood out of the water. The rock was generally clustered with birds and was called Þjóðólfur. This rock remained there until the autumn of 1936, when it vanished in calm weather one night, leaving no trace. The people of Bolungarvík remembered Þjóðólfur for a long time and knew exactly where it had been, as it had stood alone and they passed it every time they went to sea. They say that the sea is so shallow there that the rock could not lie in the sea without being seen. And so they believe that the rock vanished because the spell had reached the end of its term. Traces of where Þjóðólfur stood are clearly visible on the skerry: the rock was over five fathoms across at the base. And this is the end of the story of the siblings Þjóðólfur and Þuríður the Strait-filler, and their fate.

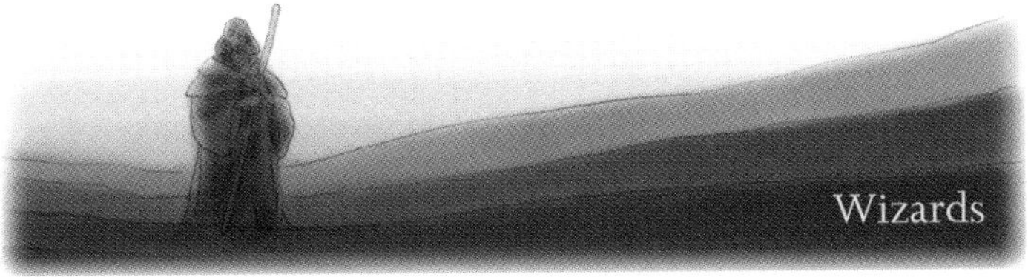

10. The Pastors of Aðalvík

North of Ísafjarðardjúp lies Aðalvík bay, open to the sea. The mountain Ritur marks the southern end of the bay, while to the north Straumnes rises, steep and majestic. The wreck of a ship, Goðafoss, which ran aground in 1916, may still be seen on the shore. Above the bay is extensive lowland, much of it verdant and picturesque. Several valleys lie inland between the mountains, the southernmost being Staðardalur. In this valley is Lake Staðarvatn, where a water-horse, or kelpie, is said to reside and play various pranks. By the lake stands a farm named Staður, a church site. On the shore by Staðardalur is Sæból, formerly a fishing centre, where a village existed at one time. Another fishing hamlet developed at Látrar, at the northern end of Aðalvík. Aðalvík was once quite densely populated, like other places in the Hornstrandir region; people lived by farming and fishing, and also exploited various other resources. Today, however, the place is deserted – the last inhabitant left in the middle of the 20th century. Yet many houses remain standing and are used by their owners in the summertime. Although Hornstrandir is far off the beaten track – mainly accessible by sea – the region attracts growing numbers of tourists, who are drawn by the magnificent natural environment. One of the many buildings that remain standing at Aðalvík is the church of Staður, a handsome edifice with a vestibule, tower and choir loft.

In past centuries many renowned clergymen served the parish of Staður in Aðalvík. One of them was Snorri

Björnsson, generally known as Snorri of Húsafell, in reference to the parish where he later served. He spent 16 years at Staður in the mid 18th century. He was believed to have supernatural skills, which came in useful in his relations with the Hornstrandir folk: Snorri generally got the better of them in such magical tricks.

A story told of Snorri when he was at Staður says that the pastor was once doing some carpentry down by the sea, while nearby a neighbour, who had supernatural skills, was also doing carpentry. This neighbour was carving runes into a rod of wood, of such a nature that anyone who read the runes would go blind. He threw the rod into the sea and let it drift to where the pastor sat. The Rev. Snorri was unaware of the trick, read the runes and immediately went blind. But Snorri was a fine poet and in this situation he made use of his poetic skills and made up verses to regain his sight. Then he scraped all the runes off the rod, flung it back in the sea, and said: "Go back to your master and you shall cause his death, if he intends to use you for evil purposes again." The farmer saw the rod and grabbed it. He planned to carve it with such powerful runes that the pastor would die. But the knife slipped off the rod and into the farmer's chest, up to the hilt. With this the farmer died, and so he got his just deserts for his attempt on the pastor's life.

The Rev. Snorri was succeeded at the parish by the Rev. Vigfús Benediktsson, who remained at Staður for 18 years. According to folklore, he was subjected to sorcery by some of his parishioners, but fortunately he had a wife who knew how to respond. The Rev. Vigfús first served the parish of Staður in Aðalvík. There were many sorcerers in the congregation, who were opposed to the pastor. One Saturday the pastor went with two brothers by boat out to an island with their lambs. When they reached the island they put the lambs ashore to graze. The pastor disembarked but the others stayed in the boat. When the pastor returned, the brothers had gone with the boat and left him behind alone. The pastor's wife was named Málfríður. She was an intelligent woman, who knew many things and was said to have magical powers. She came down to the sea when the boat arrived and asked the brothers where Vigfús was. They told her he was writing his sermon for the next day, and smirked. She replied that it was quite possible that he might address them tomorrow. Then they went their separate ways; the brothers went home and thought no more of the pastor.

Early the following day the same brothers came to church. When they entered the church the pastor was standing before the altar. He preached a fierce sermon over them, which they well deserved. After Mass Málfríður said to them: "Now you have had the sermon you need, and it serves you right." They answered that they had not yet thanked the pastor for the sermon, but they would do so another time. And all summer they never came to church, until the first Sunday of the winter. One of the brothers was a married man and sat in the choir, while the other was unmarried and sat in the nave. The pastor's wife saw that they were continually smirking at each other, and as soon as the pastor stepped into the pulpit, both brothers walked out. Some time passed. When the pastor was in the middle of his sermon, Málfríður called out to him: "Fúsi, go out; the sooner the better." The pastor immediately stopped the sermon and walked out of the church and up above the churchyard. He saw one of the brothers heating a pot, while the other was writing some magical runes. The pastor came up to them and made to empty the pot, but his wife had arrived by this time and stopped him. She took the pot and poured the contents over the head of one of the brothers, then threw the pot at the other and both fell down dead. Málfríður said afterwards that it was as well they acted at once, for the brothers had intended to kill the Rev. Vigfús in the pulpit with their sorcery.

While the Rev. Vigfús was pastor of Aðalvík, he was constantly at loggerheads with magicians and in the end he had to leave, for his life was in danger. When he served in Austur-Skaftafellssýsla [at the other end of the country], his old parishioners were always sending ghosts to plague him, but his wife could always turn them back and ensure they did not harm him. The Rev. Vigfús said that all these spells would be the death of him if he lived longer than his wife. But it did not come to that, for she survived him and he died peacefully in old age.

11. The Infamous Ghost of Snæfjöll

The stretch of coastline north of Ísafjarðardjúp is known as Snæfjallaströnd (Snowy Mountain Shore). The region is quite well vegetated, with low-growing birch in places, but the snowfall tends to be heavy there in winter and expanses of snow often remain unthawed far into the summer, some reaching right down to the seashore. In the past, Snæfjallaströnd was quite densely populated, even though there is little lowland below the mountains: there is good fishing nearby and until the beginning of the 20th century a little fishing village existed at Snæfjallastaður. At that time, the population of the rural district was about 350. Now the village is gone and the district is uninhabited, with the exception of the offshore island of Æðey.

Snæfjallastaður, often named Staður or Snæfjöll, was for centuries a church site, where the pastor of Snæfjallaströnd resided. But the last pastor at Staður retired in the middle of the 19th century and shortly afterwards the church was moved to Unaðsdalur, where it still stands today. Unaðsdalur Church was an annex of Kirkjubólsþing but then came under the parish of Vatnsfjörður, whose pastor now serves the church. The old pastor's residence at Snæfjallastaður now lies in ruins. The only building that remains is the old schoolhouse of the vanished fishing hamlet. Remnants of the old church and churchyard are clearly visible, and a memorial has now been placed on the site. This ghost story is told of the old rectory at Snæfjallaströnd:

Jón Þorleifsson was pastor at Staður from 1588 to 1615. He was a learned man and reputed to be tough. He had been married twice: his first wife was named Sesselja and they had three children together. Jón was the name of one of the sons, who lived at home with his father and stepmother. The pastor had no children with his second wife. Jón the pastor's son took a liking to a maidservant on his father's farm. One of the farmhands was also involved with her, and for this reason Jón and the farmhand were not on good terms. One day in early winter, the farmhand, who was also a shepherd, was out rounding up the sheep, but he could not bring the flock down from the mountainside due to frozen snow and slippery conditions. The pastor was not impressed with his performance, which left his work undone. He then told his son, Jón, to go after the sheep, but he was reluctant, saying that the weather was too bad. The pastor paid no attention and Jón was compelled to go against his will. He did not return from this expedition but fell to his death on the mountainside.

The story does not tell whether Jón's body was ever found or not, but soon it transpired that he did not rest in peace, as he began to haunt the maidservant and the farmhand especially. Annals recount that the place was haunted and before long the ghost grew to be a plague. He lurked on the mountainside at Snæfjöll, throwing rocks at passers-by and playing various other pranks. He was said to break windows and kill livestock at Snæfjallastaður. He often sat in the *baðstofa* (living room) during the day, while the women were spinning and knitting, and demanded to be fed like the rest of the household. And it is said that at Snæfjöll he secretly licked the inside of people's food-bowls after they had eaten. One day the farmhand heard someone tearing the skin off the fish that hung in the fish-drying shack, and saw that it was the ghost. The farmhand asked him: "Don't you want a knife, man?" And the ghost retorted at once: "Dead men need no knives. They tear and devour their prey."

One winter, there was a shortage of tobacco. Then the Rev. Jón told the ghost to go north to Eyjafjörður, for he knew that tobacco was available at Akureyri. The ghost was in the habit of running errands for the pastor, but he had to be given plenty of food for the journey. When he returned from the north, a certain man saw the ghost as he sat and ate, with tobacco scattered around him. The man said: "Good man, whoever you are, give me a taste of that tobacco." The ghost flashed his eyes ferociously, swept up the tobacco and vanished, leaving two ells [about one metre] of tobacco where he had sat.

The pastor was keen to be rid of the ghost, so he wrote to a friend, the Rev. Einar Sigurðsson at Skorrastaður in Norðfjörður, and sent the ghost east with the letter. He was sure that if anyone could rid him of this plague, it was the Rev. Einar. The ghost came to the Rev. Einar's bedside one evening, when the pastor was abed. The pastor asked if he wanted to speak to him and the ghost said yes. The pastor did not much like the look of this visitor, and when the ghost made to attack him, he grabbed his bed-board and struck the ghost's arm, so it broke in two. At that moment the ghost threw the letter to the pastor. The pastor got out of bed and suggested that the ghost return to the west, but he replied that this was the last thing he wished to do. Then the pastor pretended to be thinking of a plan that would work; he told the ghost to return to Snæfjallastaður at the end of Mass, and to be sure of meeting the Rev. Jón at the lychgate. He was to hand him a note that the Rev. Einar gave him. So the ghost was compelled to leave, although it was against his will. He met the pastor at the lychgate and handed him the note from the east. In the note was a spell to exorcise the ghost and the Rev. Jón immediately cast this spell to prevent the Snæfjöll ghost from haunting any living men or beasts, and sent him north and down to the nether ninth world. This spell was so powerful that the ghost vanished at once, and never again did any harm at Snæfjallastaður or anywhere else.

12. The Haunting of the Rev. Jón of Tröllatunga

Steingrímsfjörður is the largest fjord in the Strandir region, about 28 km long and 7 km across in its outer reaches, narrowing farther inland. The southern shore of the fjord is quite densely populated, notably in Hólmavík, a growing fishing community whose population is between four and five hundred. The northern side of the fjord is more sparsely populated, but a fishing hamlet has grown up at Drangsnes on Selströnd. From the head of Steingrímsfjörður extends Staðardalur, a grassy, picturesque valley whose name is derived from the old church site of Staður, known in former times as Breiðabólsstaður. A good-quality road leads through Staðardalur, and continues over Steingrímsfjarðarheiði to Langadalsströnd by Ísafjarðardjúp. This road has greatly improved communications for the residents of Ísafjörður and of the West Fjords in general. In the outer reaches of Steingrímsfjörður is the island of Grímsey, the largest island in the Strandasýsla region. An old legend says that some trolls once started to dig a tunnel across the neck of land between Gílsfjörður and Húnaflói. They never completed the task, but the rock they excavated from the tunnel was thrown out to sea and formed the islands of Breiðafjörður to the west and Grímsey to the east. There was once a farm on Grímsey island but it was inhabited only intermittently. Fox cubs were sometimes taken out to Grímsey to fend for themselves, as food is plentiful on the island; they were then hunted in the winter when their skins were at their most valuable.

At the south of Steingrímsfjörður, in a pleasant, verdant hollow, stands the manor of Tröllatunga. The first settler at Tröllatunga was Steingrímur, after whom Steingrímsfjörður is named. In the past, it was believed that precious metals and hidden treasure might be found on the estate of Tröllatunga. Gullhóll (Gold Hill) was once excavated but no treasure was found. The ancient rock strata at Tröllatunga are, however, rich in fossils and lignite (brown coal), which are well worth examining. There was a church at Tröllatunga until 1910 and it was a pastor's residence for centuries. One of the pastors of Tröllatunga in the early 19th century was the Rev. Björn Hjálmarsson, who is reputed to have been an excellent preacher, a versifier, a good healer, and a talented writer and painter. Among his children was a son named Jón, who received an education. He completed his studies and later served as his father's curate for some years, but died before his time. The Rev. Jón is the subject of a folk tale, which also relates to sorcerers in Arnarfjörður, who were said to be especially adept in the magic arts. The story goes something like this:

Björn Hjálmarsson was pastor for many years at Tröllatunga in Strandasýsla. One of his sons was named Jón. The Rev. Björn sent him to school and later took him on as a chaplain. The Rev. Jón was a sociable character, who mocked occultism and superstition whenever he encountered such beliefs. One summer, an Arnarfjörður man was employed on the farm at Tröllatunga, who boasted that he had supernatural skills, like many other Arnarfjörður people. When the chaplain heard this, he began to ridicule the man, asking him to demonstrate his powers, and sorely provoking him. Finally, the man grew angry and said he would send him a message that would show what he could do. The chaplain laughed at this and challenged the Arnarfjörður man to fulfil his threat. Then the man returned home and before long the Rev. Jón had forgotten the threat.

The following summer, the chaplain slept in a building on the farm, and one night in late summer he awoke when he felt something touching his quilt. The chaplain looked up and thought he saw a demon at the end of his bed. The chaplain lay down again and ignored this apparition. Then the demon reached out to him again and tickled him. The chaplain sat up and said, "Get out. You're too feeble for me to be afraid of you." Then the demon vanished, but shortly afterwards the chaplain saw that a thick cloud of fog seemed to enter the building. When it was all inside it seemed to the chaplain that it became a monster that filled the entire building. Then the chaplain said: "I'm not afraid of you. You're nothing but size alone. You will need more substance to do me harm, so get out." Then the apparition seeped out.

Now the chaplain remembered the Arnarfjörður man and his threat. He expected yet another vision to appear but he was still confident. Then suddenly an image seemed to float in through the doorway. This phenomenon glowed like fire and was in the shape of a triangle with sharp corners. At that moment it seemed to the chaplain that the whole room was filled with beds, with a man in every one, each with his chest bare. Then it seemed to the chaplain that the image glided from the doorway and stuck one corner into the chest of the man lying nearest the door. The chaplain saw the corner sink deep into the man's chest, and he cried out and died at once. Then the triangle glided to the next man and slew him in the same manner, and he also cried out at the pain. It appeared to the chaplain that the apparition did not stop until all were dead.

Finally, the image made for the chaplain himself, who jumped up stark naked from his bed, spread out his arms and said in a loud voice: "Come now, but come in the name of Jesus." And as soon as the chaplain had spoken these words, all the visions vanished and everything returned to normal. And here ends the story of the fearless chaplain of Tröllatunga.

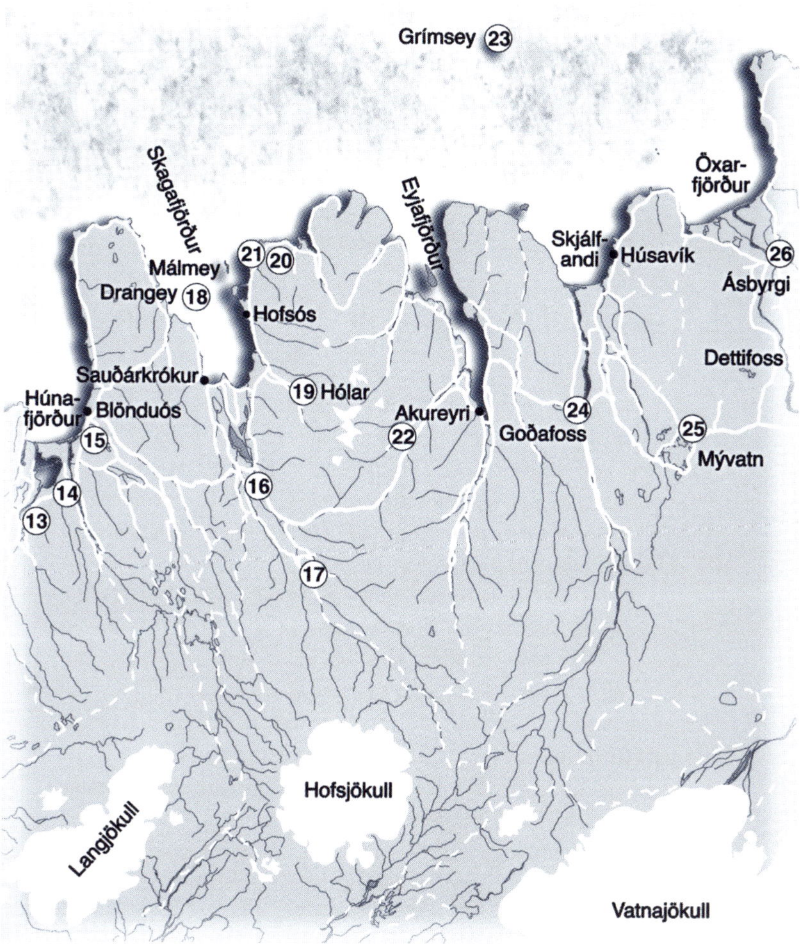

NORTH ICELAND

13. Kola of Kolugljúfur

The journey northward continues over Holtavörðuheiði, through Hrútafjörður, over Hrútafjarðarháls and down into Miðfjörður, a picturesque and fertile region. On the eastern shore of Miðfjörður is Laugarbakki, a small hamlet and educational centre. Farther inland on the same side of the river is the manor of Bjarg, the birthplace of saga hero Grettir Ásmundarson, the strongest man in Iceland in his day. A little farther east is a rocky formation named Hvítserkur (White Shirt), which rises up out of the sea just offshore from the farm of Súluvellir. The rock resembles some ancient or mythical beast, and folklore claims that it was once a night troll on his way to throw rocks at the Þingeyrar monastery. But his plans came to nothing, for he was caught in the rays of the rising sun and turned to stone.

Continuing on the Ring Road, travellers will see Borgarvirki on the left-hand side, where it rises impressively between Vesturhóp and Víðidalur. Borgarvirki (Borg Fort) consists of a columnar-basalt formation 10–15 m high, within which there is a hollow 5–6 m deep, opening out to the east. The gap has been filled with a sturdy rock wall and defences have also been built on top of the natural basalt formation in several places. This ancient structure had largely collapsed but was rebuilt in 1949–50. In the hollow above Borgarvirki there are remnants of two buildings and also traces of a well, which has totally collapsed. Ancient sources make no mention of the "fort", but it has been suggested that it was built by Barði Guðmundsson of Ásbjarnarnes, who waged a small war against the people of Borgarfjörður, according to Heiðarvíga saga (the Saga of the Killings on the Heath). An oral tradition tells how Barði's enemies once approached from the south with a large force. Barði received intelligence of this and took refuge in the fort. The Borgarfjörður army then laid siege to the fort, intending to starve Barði into submission, but he fooled them by flinging the last blood-sausage in the fort out to the besieging forces. They concluded that there was plenty of food in the fort and abandoned the siege, leaving Barði the victor. Another tradition claims that the fort was built by Finnbogi the Strong of Stóra-Borg, when he was in conflict with the Vatnsdalur folk. Yet another theory is that the structure dates from the Settlement Age (around AD 900). Whatever the truth of the matter, Borgarvirki is one of Iceland's oldest and most remarkable man-made structures, unique in the country.

Beyond Borgarvirki, a right turn off the Ring Road leads into the valley of Víðidalur, an attractive region rich in history. Víðidalstunga, a famous old manor, stands on a tongue of land between the Víðidalsá and Fitjá rivers. It was here that Flateyjarbók (the Flatey Book), a large and beautifully illuminated book of saga manuscripts, was compiled for the magnate Jón Hákonarson in around 1400. Vellum prepared from 113 calfskins was required to make the book, which eventually made its way to the island of Flatey in Breiðafjörður, west Iceland – hence its name. Flateyjarbók was presented to Bishop Brynjólfur Sveinsson of Skálholt when he visited the island in 1647, and he in turn gave it to King Frederick II of Denmark. After about three centuries in Copenhagen, this national treasure was returned to Iceland in 1971, along with another priceless manuscript, the Codex Regius of Eddic verse, after the Danes had agreed to return most of their collection of Old Icelandic manuscripts.

Víðidalstunga was inhabited for centuries by the same family, and during a period when the social elite started to imitate foreign custom by adopting family names instead of traditional patronymics, the family began to call themselves Vídalín, a surname derived from the name of the valley, Víðidalur. The Vídalín family included various renowned men, such as Páll Vídalín, who with Professor Árni Magnússon carried out a survey and census in the early 18th century, and Bishop Jón Vídalín, author of the "Vídalín Homilies", published in 1718, which was probably the most widely read book in Iceland well into the 20th century.

Beyond the Fitjá river with its attractive Kerafossar waterfalls, and a little farther south along the valley from the Víðidalsá river, stands the farm of Kolugil. A short walk from Kolugil, the Víðidalsá river forms two spectacular cascades in a narrow gully, Kolugljúfur. The gully is about a kilometre in length and 40–50 m deep, with vertical rock walls in many places. Kolugljúfur is named after a gigantic troll-wife, Kola, who lived there once upon a time. To the west of the farm of Kolugil is a bridge over the river, which commands an excellent view of this remarkable natural phenomenon, that can also be seen from the edges of the gully, on either side. This is the tale of the troll-wife Kola:

A short distance from the farm of Kolugil is a great gully, named Kola's Gully. In olden times, a huge woman named Kola is said to have lived there, and it is named after her. On the western side of the gully is a grassy hollow, still called Kolurúm (Kola's Bed), and this is where Kola is said to have lain at night when she wanted to sleep. At the front of the hollow are two thin rock pillars, which are called Bríkur (Bedposts). Between them is a gap, below which there is a cliff down to the Víðidalsá river, which flows through the gully. When Kola wanted her breakfast, it is said that she reached down through the gap and into the river for salmon.

At the farm of Kolugil is a hill called Kola's Hill, beneath which Kola is supposed to be buried. Attempts have often been made to dig up the hill but these have always been abandoned for one reason or another: once, the church at Víðidalstunga appeared to be on fire; another time, the river appeared to be flowing up the bank below Kolugil towards the farmhouse. Now there is a hollow in the hill, which is said to be two to three ells across [an ell is about 50 cm].

That is the story of the troll-wife Kola, and though she is long gone from Víðidalur, it is well worth visiting the valley and seeing her old stamping ground.

14. The Skíðastaðir Girl and the Raven

The Ring Road leads eastwards through Húnavatnssýsla district, via Hrútafjörður and Miðfjörður, Línakradalur and Víðidalur. At the mouth of the Vatnsdalur valley is a vast collection of hillocks, the famous Vatnsdalshólar (Vatnsdalur Hillocks), which are said to be innumerable, like the islands of Breiðafjörður or the lakes of Arnarvatnsheiði. The origins of the hillocks are not clear, but the commonly held view is that they were formed by a huge slide of rock from Mt. Vatnsdalsfjall in prehistoric times.

South of the hillocks is a large lake, Flóðið, which formed in 1720 when a landslide struck the farm of Bjarnastaðir, killing six people. The landslide dammed the river, forming a new lake. Through the valley flows the Vatnsdalsá, one of Iceland's most picturesque and teeming salmon rivers, formed by the confluence of many smaller rivers that flow off the highlands to fall in a series of waterfalls through a large gully in the inner reaches of the valley.

Vatnsdalur was first settled by Ingimundur Þorsteinsson the Aged, who made his home at Hof. He was attracted by the beauty of the valley, and by its excellent resources of woods and grasslands. On the way to this new home, Ingimundur's wife bore him a daughter, Þórdís, who is said to have been the first native of the Húnavatnssýsla area. She was born at Vatnsdalshólar, where a monument has now been raised to her, along with a wood named Þórdísarlundur (Þórdís's Grove) in her honour. To the west of the wood is Flóðvangur, a community centre providing accommodation for anglers in the Vatnsdalsá river. Many landslides have fallen from the slopes of Mt. Vatnsdalsfjall *to the east of the valley, leaving traces on the slopes and lowlands beneath. In addition to the Bjarnastaðir landslide mentioned above, an even larger landslide fell in 1545, laying waste to the farm of Skíðastaðir. Thirteen people died, but tradition says that one girl survived in an extraordinary manner:*

Long ago at Skíðastaðir there lived a very wealthy farmer. He had many labourers on his farm and kept them hard at work both winter and summer. During the haymaking season he had the women servants cook meals only on Sundays, so that they could help with the haymaking on other days, and he would permit his workers neither to attend church nor to read the Good Book at home. Early one Sunday morning, a man dressed in white, and carrying a staff in his hand, was seen from many farms in the area as he walked northwards over Vatnsdalsfjall. He halted above Skíðastaðir and struck the mountain with his staff. Immediately a landslide began there, which grew larger and larger as it slipped down the slope. This awesome rockslide struck the farmhouse of Skíðastaðir, so that no living person survived except for one girl, who was at that moment away from the farmhouse.

This girl had been at Skíðastaðir for a long time, although she was not happy there and was dissatisfied with the farmer's godlessness. But she was kind and willing, and for this she was popular both with her masters and with the other workers. She often had to cook on holy days and received no extra reward, except that she was allowed to scrape the pot. The winter before the landslide fell was very harsh, so that both people and beasts died of starvation. The farmer of Skíðastaðir had plenty of everything but he refused to share it with others, though he was asked to do so, and he cruelly turned away all those who came in search of help. The girl, who cooked on Sundays, was sad not to be able to help the poor and hungry people, and she tried to give them some of her own food and the scrapings of the pots. The harsh winter was also difficult for all animals that had to be outside, so that they lay dead in piles. And crowds of ravens collected at farms to peck at any refuse that might be thrown out. The girl threw out as much as she could from the kitchen, for she was kind of heart and wanted to help the ravens, like the others. One of the ravens grew so fond of her that he followed her every step out of doors. In the spring and summer following that harsh winter, he arrived early every morning at Skíðastaðir, for the girl always kept some food for him.

On the Sunday morning of the landslide, the girl had risen very early to cook porridge. She hurried to finish scraping out the pot before the raven arrived, so that she could give him the scrapings. Just as she was finishing, she heard the raven croak outside. She took the scrapings outside in a ladle and placed them on the stones where she normally fed the bird. But the raven would not touch his food. He fluttered around and then flew a little distance out into the field. The girl followed with her ladle, but he did not want to eat there and flew farther off. So it continued: the girl followed the raven, trying to feed him, but he always flew up and went farther and farther away. The girl did not understand why the raven was behaving so strangely but she was determined to feed him. She followed him until he had led her some distance south of the homefield. The girl started to think that this was enough, that she must run back to the farmhouse. But at that moment she heard a roaring in the mountain, which preceded the landslide and the flood of water that accompanied it, and she saw this mass sweep over the farmhouse and right across the valley. And she thanked God with all her heart for sending the wise raven to save her.

15. The Reaper of Tindar

The Ring Road to the north is an easy drive, but there is so much to see along the way that it is worth stopping here and there to look around. The road descends from Holtavörðuheiði into Hrútafjörður by way of Grænumýrartunga, which was once the southernmost habitation in the Strandasýsla region. Formerly a thriving farm where many travellers stopped on their journeys, the place is now abandoned. Following the eastern shore of Hrútafjörður, the road passes the Staðarskáli roadhouse, a popular meal stop. Farther out along the fjord is Reykjaskóli (Reykir School), formerly a regional school centre for the West Húnavatnssýsla and Strandir areas, but now closed down. At the old school there is now a folk museum which is worth visiting; it houses the shark-fishing vessel Ófeigur, from Ófeigsfjörður in the Strandir region, along with various other items from the days when sharks, like whales, were hunted for their valuable oil. After crossing Hrútafjarðarháls, the road comes down into Miðfjörður between Heggstaðanes in the west and Vatnsnes in the east. A short distance out along the fjord is the village of Hvammstangi, and much farther out the farm of Illugastaðir. This was the home of Natan Ketilsson, who was murdered there in 1828, along with a guest in the house, Pétur Jónsson. The killers set the farmhouse on fire to conceal their crime but they were discovered all the same. Among them were Friðrik Sigurðsson and Agnes Magnúsdóttir, who were beheaded at Vatnsdalshólar in 1830 – Iceland's last execution.

In the north of the Vatnsnes peninsula is the farm of Hindisvík, which was a sanctuary for seals and seabirds for many years, thanks to the efforts of the Rev. Sigurður Norland, who served the parish of Tjörn. A road circles Vatnsnes, and much of interest may be seen along this route, for instance the strangely shaped offshore rock Hvítserkur, which rises up out of Húnafjörður to the east of the headland.

Further east is the valley of Víðidalur, where the Víðidalsá river meanders attractively among green meadows. To the east of the river, in the outer reaches of the valley, is the farm of Lækjamót. The first Christian missionaries to visit Iceland, Bishop Fridrik and Þorvaldur the Far-Travelled, stayed at Lækjamót in the late 10th century. They met with fierce resistance from heathen Icelanders, some of whom gathered forces to attack the farm, intending to burn the companions to death. But just as their forces were approaching the farmhouse, a flock of birds flew up, startling the horses, so that many of the men were thrown and injured. The attack was, of course, abandoned.

Continuing through Vatnsdalshólar, the road passes Stóra Giljá, which was the family home of the missionary Þorvaldur the Far-Travelled. A short distance above the farm's homefield is a rock known as Gullsteinn (Gold Rock). Þorvaldur's father, Koðrán, was a heathen who attributed special powers to the Gold Rock, where he believed his guardian-spirit resided. When the missionaries sang Mass over the rock it split open, and Koðrán saw that the God in whom his son believed was a mighty god, and agreed to be baptised. A monument has been raised here to these first missionaries and a cross has been placed near the road. Another reminder of early Christianity is at nearby Þingeyrar, on the lowlands beyond the Húnavatn lake; this was the site of Iceland's first monastery, founded in 1133.

After crossing the Giljá river, whose source is in Sauðadalur between Svínadalur and Vatnsdalsfjöll, we reach the district generally known as Ásar. This stretches south from Blönduós, the main town of Húnavatnssýsla, between the river Blanda and Lake Húnavatn. It is a rather low-lying area with few landmarks, through which the river Laxá á Ásum (also known as Neðri Laxá or Lower Salmon River) flows – one of the most expensive salmon rivers in Iceland. The river flows out of the Laxárvatn lake and into the sea at Húnaós. The Fremri Laxá (Upper Salmon River), on the other hand, flows out of Lake Svínavatn and into Lake Laxárvatn, hence contributing to the water-flow of the lower river. This valuable river was harnessed at an early date to *supply Blönduós and nearby rural areas with electricity. The Ásar area boasts many fine farms, as the soil makes for good grassland. One of these farms is Tindar, which is known for the following folk tale:*

Once upon a time there was a farmer at Tindar in Húnavatnssýsla named Árni Þorleifsson. He was an excellent farmer who also had some supernatural skills. One summer the grass in the fields was growing poorly due to cold weather and drift-ice close to the shore. Farmer Árni left his hayfields unmown during the summer in order to allow the grass to grow as much as possible. Others mowed their grass as usual, but even when they had finished their haymaking, Árni had not yet started to mow his grass. Shortly after this he asked the Devil to mow the grass on the homefield for him, in a single night. The Devil asked what his reward would be and the farmer said he might name his own fee. Then the Devil said he wanted the farmer himself in return. Árni agreed, on condition that the Devil mowed the whole field in a single night and finished before Árni rose in the morning.

The homefield at Tindar was very stony and in one place at the bottom of the field there was a rocky ruin known as Gníputótt. This was said to have been a chapel in former times and it was not possible to swing a scythe there without hitting a rock. Shortly after this, Árni prepared many scythes with sharpened blades. That evening he told the household to lie still and not move during the night. They did as he said, except for one old woman. She wanted to know what was going on, got out of bed and peeked out through the farmhouse door, which was open a crack. She saw a demon on every tussock and immediately went blind in the eye that had looked out; soon afterwards she went mad.

In the morning when the farmer came out, the Devil had mowed all the homefield except for the ruins mentioned before. He was struggling to cut the grass there and his scythe had grown blunt. When Árni went to him, the Devil was chanting this verse to himself:

> At Gníputótt wherever I wield
> the scythe-iron it strikes on stone.
> Though Tindar is a slender field
> it's tardy work for one.

He had mown all the grass but for two tussocks in Gníputótt. On one Árni had placed the Bible and on the other a book of Psalms, and the Devil eschewed such literature. Árni then said that the agreement was void, and told the Devil to go away and never come back. Gníputótt still bears the same name, and traces of it may be seen in the homefield at Tindar; below it is a marsh. It is clear that the wall around the homefield was formerly below the ruins, which were thus inside the homefield, as the story says.

16. Solveig and the Reverend Oddur

An impressive and beautiful view meets travellers crossing the Vatnsskarð pass to the east into the history-steeped territory of Skagafjörður. Arnarstapi, where a memorial stands to the Icelandic-Canadian "Rocky Mountain Poet" Stephan G. Stephansson, is a good place to stop and enjoy the view. To the left one can see as far as Mt. Tindastóll and the islands of the fjord, while on the right rises Mt. Mælifellshnjúkur, whose clean-cut peak is outlined against the sky. Straight ahead, in the east, lie the splendid Blönduhlíðarfjöll mountains, rising to a height of more than 1,000 m. The area beneath these mountains, stretching west to the Héraðsvötn river, is a fertile and relatively densely populated rural district called Blönduhlíð. Close to the main road in the middle of this community is Miklibær, a manor famous in Icelandic history and the site of a church and rectory for many centuries. In the churchyard at Miklibær there is a monument on the grave of folk poet Bólu-Hjálmar (Hjálmar of Bóla, 1796–1875). Historically, Miklibær is connected with such famous events as the 13th-century Battle of Örlygsstaðir, one of the bloodiest battles of the bloody Sturlung Age. And in the 15th century, the Rev. Sigmundur Steinþórsson led an attack on Miklibær as part of his dispute with the Bishop of Hólar.

But Miklibær is probably best known for the 18th-century folk tale of an unfortunate girl named Solveig, who committed suicide in 1778, and the Rev. Oddur Gíslason, who vanished without trace in 1786. The tale is as follows:

A girl named Solveig was employed in the household of the Rev. Oddur Gíslason of Miklibær. She fell in love with the pastor and wanted him to marry her, but he was not of the same mind. She went mad as a result and was determined to kill herself. So the people of the household watched over her, particularly a woman named Guðlaug Björnsdóttir, the sister of the Rev. Snorri of Húsafell, who kept watch over her at night. One day at dusk, however, Solveig escaped her vigilance and made her way out to some ruins in the homefield. Þorsteinn, a farmhand in the pastor's employ, followed her but she was so quick that by the time he reached her she had cut her throat. When Þorsteinn saw the blood pouring from her throat, he is supposed to have said, "Now the Devil's got her." He heard Solveig mutter something, and he understood her to mean that he should give a message to the pastor, that he should allow her to lie in the churchyard. Having spoken these words, she expired.

Þorsteinn told the household what had happened, and gave the pastor Solveig's message, with her request to be allowed to lie in hallowed ground. The pastor applied to his superiors for permission but was denied, as the girl had taken her own life. The night after the pastor was refused, he dreamed that Solveig came to him and said: "Since you will not allow me a place in hallowed ground, you shall not lie there either," with an expression of anger on her face. After this, Solveig was buried outside the churchyard and without rites. Shortly afterwards, she began to haunt the Rev. Oddur when he was out alone, whether he was riding to the church at Silfrastaðir or elsewhere. This came to be known throughout the region and every man made it his duty to escort the pastor home if he was out late.

One day the Rev. Oddur rode to the Silfrastaðir church, and by the end of the day he had not returned. The household had no fears for his safety, since they knew that he was always escorted home when he was late. And so it was on that occasion: the pastor was escorted home as far as the homefield at Miklibær. There he told his companion that he need not escort him farther, as he would reach home safely, and they parted. That evening, the household people at Miklibær heard someone knocking at the outside door but because they felt the knock at the door was strange they did not answer it. Then they heard someone go up onto the *baðstofa* (living room) roof in haste, but before the person there could knock at the window, he was hauled down as if someone was pulling at his legs. When they looked out later that evening, they saw that the pastor's horse was outside the farmhouse, with his gloves and whip tucked into the saddle. They grew most uneasy over this, for they saw that the pastor had come home but was now vanished without trace. They started to search for him, asking after him at every farm where he might have gone, and they were told that he had been accompanied as far as the homefield that evening, but that he had not wanted to be escorted farther. After this, search parties were formed and searched for him continuously for many days without success. Finally, the search was abandoned, and the general opinion was that Solveig had made good her threat, ensuring that the Rev. Oddur would not lie in the churchyard by dragging him down into her own grave. But her grave was never opened to look.

This is the folk tale of Solveig and the Rev. Oddur. Various other tales exist about the vanished pastor. It has been suggested that his body was actually discovered and secretly buried, perhaps in Héraðsdalur, where there was a graveyard at that time, but this has never been proved, and the disappearance of the Rev. Oddur has always been regarded as a great mystery. It is the subject of a famous poem by Einar Benediktsson (1864–1940), *Hvarf séra Odds frá Miklabæ* (the Disappearance of the Rev. Oddur from Miklibær).

17. *Wether-Snorri of Þorljótsstaðir*

From the main region of Skagafjörður, three valleys cut southwards into the highlands, the central one named Vesturdalur (West Valley). On the way to Skagafjörður, a turning southwards off the Ring Road, a short distance south of the hamlet of Varmahlíð, leads through Tungusveit, over Goðdalaháls and into Vesturdalur. In the outer reaches of the valley are low grassy ridges, with considerable lowland, but farther south the mountains grow higher and the valley narrows. Vesturdalur is a thriving agricultural district with many farms. There were once many more, however, especially in the inner reaches of the valley, but they have left little trace besides place-names. At the innermost end of the valley, only about 20 km north of the Hofsjökull glacier, is a deserted place that is steeped in legend and mystery – Hraunþúfuklaustur (Lava Tussock Priory) or simply Klaustur. This is reputed to have been a religious house in former times: some say a monastery, others a convent. Traces of old buildings may be seen there and it is said that long ago a church bell, a chalice and a door-ring were unearthed there, which were given to the church at Goðdalir.

A short distance above Hraunþúfuklaustur is Hraunþúfugil (Lava Tussock Gully), where two folk tales tell of a place-name connected with the reputed religious house. Hraunþúfa is the name of a high rocky ridge on the southern side of the gully. According to tradition, the abbot once took his shepherd boy, Holofernis, up on to the rock, where the boy helped him bury a valuable hoard of silver. After this the abbot is supposed to have taken the boy up on to another cliff on the northern side of the gully and pushed him off the edge, so that he *could not tell where the treasure was buried. Since then the cliff has been named Holofernishöfði (Holofernis' Headland). Another tale of this Holofernis is that he was a shepherd with the nuns at Hraunþúfuklaustur. He had a hard life, for every morning the abbess tied a cream churn on his back and he was not allowed to return until the cream was churned into butter. He had to look after the sheep all day with this burden on his back. Finally, the shepherd had enough of serving the cruel nuns and jumped off a cliff on the northern side of Hraunþúfugil, which has been called Holofernishöfði ever since.*

Þorljótsstaðir was the innermost habitation in Vesturdalur in recent centuries, until the farm was abandoned shortly before 1950. Þorljótsstaðir appears to have been inhabited from the early days of Icelandic history in the 10th century, as an ancient heathen burial site was discovered near the farmhouse. For many years this was the most remote habitation in Iceland but today, after being abandoned, it is more accessible than ever before, as a car track has been cleared over Mt. Þorljótsstaðafjall, southeast across the highland plateau to Laugafell, and to Fjórðungavatn, where it meets the Sprengisandur route across the highlands.

Þorljótsstaðir is connected with a folk tale of the farmer Snorri, who owned so many sheep that he was known as Wether-Snorri [a "wether" is a gelded ram]:

There was a man named Snorri who was known as Wether-Snorri. He lived at Þorljótsstaðir, shortly after the Black Death. He had many sheep, which he left out in winter at Þorljótsstaðaruna, which is the name given to the eastern side of the valley as far as Hraunþúfuklaustur. Once there was a very harsh winter. Snorri's herd included two rather good bellwethers. Between the New Year and Twelfth Night, all Snorri's sheep disappeared and he could not find them, however much he searched. But when the snow melted in the spring, all the sheep were back in their usual place. The next winter was also a hard one. Snorri decided to take better care of his sheep, and went out to them, taking a piece of good fat tripe with him. He reached the place that is still called Snorrasteinn (Snorri's Rock), near Klaustur, where there had been a farm before the Black Death. He sat on the rock and ate the tripe. His sheep were then west of the river, to the south of Hraunþúfugil.

When Snorri made to head the sheep off, they went up on to Hraunþúfurani and into the lava field. Snorri followed, but could not head them off, as there was heavy drifting snow. It is said that they went to the east of the Ásbjarnarvötn lakes, which are reputed to have been good fishing lakes, east of Lambahraun and Illviðrishnjúkar, and then east of the Hofsjökull glacier. Snorri followed them for nearly a day and a half, after which he reached a grass field that had been mown. Then he saw a sheep shed. A man stood in the doorway and said, upon seeing the sheep: "So you're back again, you poor beasts." When Snorri asked if he had seen them before, the man told him that they had sheltered there the previous winter. Snorri asked where he was. "Hamarsholt in Hreppar," replied the man, who was a farmer there. [In other words, the sheep had found their way across the entire highland plateau to the south of Iceland.] Snorri spent a comfortable winter with him, and on Good Friday his sheep set off northwards across the mountains, the same way they had come, and Snorri went with them. He arrived home at Þorljótsstaðir on the evening of Easter Saturday. He entered the kitchen, where he found a dish of meat on the hearth, took a piece and ate it. At that moment his wife entered the building, saw Snorri and fainted, taking him for a ghost. He bent over her and when she regained consciousness they were delighted to see each other again. Snorri is said to have rewarded the farmer of Hamarsholt well for the winter grazing.

It is said that there was once a church at Klaustur, as mentioned above. There is excellent grazing for horses there, and a staging post for men who round up sheep in the Lambatungur area. Some of them were once wrestling there, as they do, and one fell on his knee. He felt a sharp point in the earth and when it was examined it was the colour of verdigris. When it was dug up, it turned out to be a bell. At Hraunþúfurani is a cave with room for six men, which is called Bjartabaðstofa (Bright *baðstofa* or living room).

18. Somewhere for the Wicked

There are many places of interest along the route to the north, but nothing compares with crossing the *Vatnsskarð* pass and descending into the Skagafjörður district, with history at every step. To the east are the Blönduhlíðarfjöll mountains, with Mt. Glóðafeykir in the middle; to the north stands Mt. Tindastóll, surrounded by cliffs. And from the blue depths of the fjord rise the islands of Drangey and Málmey, while the headland of Þórðarhöfði stands guard over the fjord's eastern shore. To the south is Mt. Mælifellshnjúkur, the "sacred mountain" of the region. A patch of snow generally remains on the mountain long into the spring, in the shape of a horse. In times past, when the snow-image of the horse had parted at the withers, the local farmers took it as a sign that the mountain route to the south was open, so that they could set off to buy new supplies of stockfish.

On the way down from *Vatnsskarð*, there is a memorial to Stephan G. Stephansson, the Icelandic-Canadian "Rocky-Mountain Poet", who was born in 1853 at Kirkjuhóll near *Víðimýri*. The memorial, conceived by sculptor Ríkarð Jónsson, was built by local people on the centenary of the poet's birth. Stephan, who wrote in Icelandic, remained a true Icelander even though he emigrated to the New World as a very young man.

In the middle of the region is the hamlet of *Varmahlíð*, where all the Skagafjörður roads come together. One of these leads to Sauðárkrókur, the main town in the region, with a population of over 2,000. The community's economy is based on the fisheries, commerce, industry and services. Tourism plays an important role. Among *the tourist services available are organised tours to Drangey island. The island is located on the western side of the fjord, and is formed of perpendicular basalt, 180 m high. The rock can only be scaled at one point, known as Uppganga; the ascent is quite difficult, and at the top visitors must climb a metal ladder. At the top the island is about 0.2 km² in area, almost flat and very grassy. In the past, sheep were often pastured on the island, and the grass was also mown for hay. But Drangey is best known for its vast population of seabirds. Over the centuries, Skagafjörður people caught birds and gathered eggs in vast quantities: it is said that over 200,000 birds were sometimes caught there in a single spring, and the island was generally known as "Skagafjörður's pantry".*

Drangey was never permanently inhabited but, according to the Saga of Grettir, *in 1028–30 Grettir Ásmundarson and his brother Illugi survived on the island as outlaws until they were finally slain there. When the brothers' fire went out on the island, Grettir is said to have swum ashore to Reykir, a distance of nearly 7 km, to fetch embers.*

There are many folk tales connected with Drangey. One tells of the origins of the island: two night trolls, who lived at Hegranes, were taking their cow to be serviced by a bull, for which they had to go all the way west to Strandir. They set off on their journey, the troll leading the cow, and the troll-wife walking behind. But they had only gone a short distance out into the fjord when dawn broke in the east and they were all turned to stone. The troll-wife is the rock pillar named Kerling (Old Woman) at the south of the island, and the male troll was another rock pillar, known as Karl (Old Man), which stood at the north of Drangey until it collapsed in an earthquake in 1755. The island, of course, is the troll cow.

Many lives have been lost on Drangey, as climbing the cliffs to catch birds and gather eggs was a hazardous pursuit. But long ago, people began to feel that there was something suspicious about the number of accidents on the cliffs, and it appeared that the climbing ropes had been severed by an axe or some other sharp weapon. These events were attributed to monsters or rock-dwellers who did not want humans from the mainland trespassing on their stocks of birds and eggs. This belief led to a decline in the utilisation of Drangey's resources.

In the early 13th century, Guðmundur Arason was Bishop of Hólar. He was a benefactor of the poor and other unfortunates, and was thus known as Gvendur the Good [Gvendur is a diminutive of Guðmundur]. He was renowned for blessing and consecrating many places in Iceland, including various wells, which are still known as Gvendarbrunnar (Gvendur's Wells).

The good bishop heard of the lives being lost on Drangey, which was in the possession of the episcopate of Hólar. He wanted to help, so he made his way to the island with his clergymen and holy water. On the way up on to the island he sang Mass at a rock shelf, which has been known since then as Gvendur's Altar. Everyone who visits Drangey says a prayer there. Now the bishop began to consecrate the bird cliffs with song, holy water and prayer. All went well until he arrived west of the northern end of the island. He was lowered on a rope there and began to bless the cliff, but he had not been speaking for long when a hairy grey paw emerged from the rock face, holding a sharp sword. The arm began to saw away at the rope where the bishop sat and two strands parted. But the bishop's life was saved because the third strand held fast – for it had been thoroughly consecrated. As this happened, a voice thundered from the rock: "No more blessing, Bishop Gvendur. Leave somewhere for the wicked." The bishop stopped his blessing and had himself pulled up to the cliff top. Thus a part of the cliffs was left unconsecrated. This place is called Heiðnaberg (Heathens' Cliff), and there are said to be more birds there than anywhere else on Drangey.

19. The Schooldays of Loftur the Magician

Hólar in Hjaltadalur, to the east of Skagafjörður, was for centuries one of the most important centres of power and culture in Iceland. Hólar stands in the middle of the Hjaltadalur valley, on a cluster of small hills formed by a slide of rock from Mt. Hólabyrða, the 1,244 m peak above Hólar. In 1106 the bishopric of North Iceland was established at Hólar; its first bishop, Jón Ögmundsson, later became an Icelandic saint. Bishop Jón founded a school at Hólar and paved the way for the establishment of Iceland's first monastery. Later bishops of Hólar included the renowned Guðmundur the Good, who is reputed to have consecrated wells, bird cliffs and dangerous paths all over Iceland. Jón Arason, the last Catholic bishop of Hólar, was executed in 1550 in the turmoil of the Reformation. Bishop Guðbrandur Þorláksson had an Icelandic translation of the Bible printed at Hólar in 1584.

Hólar Cathedral is one of Iceland's oldest stone buildings, consecrated in 1763, and many bishops of Hólar lie buried beneath the church floor. The cathedral possesses two crucifixes, an altarpiece that was a gift from Bishop Jón Arason, and a baptismal font made by Guðmundur Guðmundsson of Bjarnastaðahlíð, who built a great timber cathedral at Skálholt for Bishop Brynjólfur Sveinsson in the 17th century.

In 1801 the bishoprics of Hólar and Skálholt were abolished, and a single bishop of all Iceland, resident in Reykjavík, was appointed. After that, Hólar was merely a farm, served for a time by a pastor, *until in 1882 an agricultural school was founded there, which remains active today. And the former episcopal centre is now the seat of the suffragan bishop of Hólar.*

Over the centuries, innumerable boys have sat in class at Hólar and gone on to serve as pastors. Most of them performed their duties admirably, although there were exceptions, like a certain Loftur, called "the Magician", who is well known in folklore:

Loftur was a pupil at Hólar. He practised magic and urged his classmates to do the same, although they did little more than dabble. Loftur played many wicked tricks with his magic. One day he went home for the Christmas holiday: he took one of the maidservants of the place, fitted her with horseshoes and a bridle, and rode her home and back again by magic. After this the girl lay ill for a long time from wounds and exhaustion, but she could tell no one of it while Loftur lived. He got another maidservant with child and killed her with spells.

Þorleifur Skaftason was pastor at Hólar Cathedral. He often upbraided Loftur but to little effect. Loftur even played some tricks on the pastor, though without harming him, for the pastor had his own magical skills. Loftur learned all that was written in the *Gráskinna* (Greyskin) book of sorcery, but this was not enough for him. He wanted to gain access to the famous *Rauðskinna* (Redskin) book of sorcery, which belonged to Bishop Gottskálk the Cruel, who had taken it with him to the grave. Once, in early winter, Loftur spoke to one of his schoolmates, whom he knew to be brave, and asked him to help awaken some of the ancient bishops. This boy was to stand by the bell-rope and ring the bell when he received the signal. The lad agreed reluctantly, for Loftur threatened to kill him if he refused.

And so it was agreed, and on the chosen night they rose and went out into the church. The night was moonlit, so the interior of the church was fairly bright. The boy stood beneath the bells, while Loftur went to the pulpit and began to pronounce his incantations. Soon the ancient bishops rose from their graves, one after the other. They were dressed in white robes, with a cross on their breast and a staff in their hands. No sorcery was to be found among them, so Loftur redoubled his efforts, chanting the Psalms backwards in honour of the Devil. Then a thunderous noise was heard, and Gottskálk the Cruel himself rose up. He held a staff in his left hand and a red book in his right. He jeered: "You sing well, my son, but you shan't have my Redskin." Loftur chanted spells as never before, speaking both the Lord's Prayer and the Blessing backwards in honour of the Devil.

The whole church groaned and trembled. Gottskálk reluctantly held out to Loftur one corner of the book, and he reached out to take it. The boy took this for the signal he had been waiting for and rang the bell wildly. All vanished into the floor with a great noise, and Loftur was left alone, dazed and confused. Then he stumbled out to find his accomplice. After this Loftur appeared to believe that he was doomed. He could never bear to be alone and he had to have a light when darkness fell. He was often heard to say: "On the fourth Sunday of Lent I shall be in Hell and torment."

Finally, it was resolved to send him to a god-fearing pastor at Staðarstaður, who had a reputation for curing the mad and victims of sorcery. Loftur improved considerably. The fourth Sunday of Lent came around and the pastor was called out to minister to a dying neighbour. As soon as the pastor had left, Loftur rose from his bed and went to the next farm, where he persuaded a villainous old man to go out with him in a fishing boat. They went a short distance from the shore, in calm, fine weather, yet the boat was never seen or heard of again. Later a certain man said that he had seen a hairy, grey hand reach up out of the sea, grab the prow of the boat, and drag both men and vessel down into the depths.

20. The Merchant of Búðarbrekkur

Stark mountain ranges and the islands of Drangey and Málmey contribute much to the landscape of Skagafjörður. The majestic appearance of the region is further enhanced by the lofty, cliff-bound headland of Þórðarhöfði, on the eastern shore of the fjord. The headland is named after Þórður Bjarnarson, who made his home at Höfði on Höfðaströnd during the Settlement Age, and was known as Höfða-Þórður (Þórður of the Headland). His grandson was Þorfinnur karlsefni, who married Guðríður Þorbjarnardóttir and settled in Vínland (North America) in the 11th century. They remained there for some years and their son Snorri was born there; he is said to have been the first European child born in the New World. Due to conflict with the indigenous inhabitants, the family did not stay long on that distant continent but returned to Iceland, where Snorri became a farmer at Glaumbær in Skagafjörður.

Þórðarhöfði stands close to the main road, a short distance north of Hofsós. It is very prominent on the left-hand side of the route north along Höfðaströnd to Siglufjörður and Ólafsfjörður. On the inland side of Þorðarhöfði lies Höfðavatn, teeming with fish, which at 10 km² in area is the largest lake in Skagafjörður. Gravel isthmuses on either side of the lake link the headland to the mainland. Through the southern isthmus, Bæjarmöl, water flows out of the lake, and sometimes large quantities of fish swim through the channel. A long time ago there were plans to build a harbour at Þórðarhöfði and turn it into a fishing port; the poet Jóhann Sigurjónsson was one of the main proponents of the idea, but after his death in 1919 the plan was abandoned.

Þórðarhöfði is an ancient volcano, with a crater in its summit. It is 202 m high and about 5 km^2 in area. Its highest peak is Herkonuklettur (Amazon Rock), a name that recalls stories of trolls. Two hollows on the headland are called Skessuspor (Troll-wife's Footprints): a certain troll-wife at Strandir once took a shortcut across Skagafjörður to visit her sister at Hvanndalabjörg. She landed in front of the headland, leaving the footprints that can still be seen there today. On the southern side of the headland is Búðarbrekkur. Several basalt rocks stand there, which are said to be a church, shop and dwelling-place of the elves. A folk tale tells of a farmer from Þrastarstaðir, who went there on a trading trip:

At Þrastarstaðir on Höfðaströnd there lived a man named Þórður, who was regarded as rather a strange character. One winter's day he set off for the market town of Hofsós. Snow was falling so thickly that it seemed impossible to find one's way, yet Þórður set off with his sack of goods southwards across the marshes above Hofsós. But he soon lost his way in the blizzard and remained lost all that day until evening. Then all at once he thought he saw shops with goods for sale close by, such tall buildings that he was astonished. Through one window he saw people dancing and heard music playing. He knocked at the door, and a man in a greatcoat came out and asked what he wanted. Þórður told him he was lost and asked for shelter, if possible. The man said that he could be accommodated and added: "Come indoors with your sack of goods. I shall trade with you tomorrow and you will find it no worse than at Hofsós." The man in the coat then led Þórður into a room where a woman, children and servants were gathered, all in finery. The man whispered to his wife that they had a visitor who was lost and tired, and asked her to prepare something good for him. She immediately fetched plenty of good food, while the master of the house brought a bottle of wine and two glasses. He poured wine into both glasses, drank one himself and invited Þórður to drink the other. He did so, and found the wine to be the best he had ever tasted in his life. He drank one glass after another, thoroughly enjoyed himself and became quite tipsy. Finally, he was offered a comfortable bed and slept through the night.

In the morning he was given a good breakfast, after which the master of the house invited him to come to his shop to do business. Þórður sold him the goods he had brought, and the merchant paid him twice the price he normally received at Hofsós. The shop contained all sorts of merchandise, at half the price of the Hofsós shop. Þórður bought grain, linen and various other goods to fill his sack. Finally, the merchant gave him a shawl for his wife and bread for his children, and told him that this was his reward for helping his son when he was in mortal danger. Þórður said he did not remember doing any such thing, but the merchant told him the following tale:

"One day you were with a group of other men below Þórðarhöfði, waiting for a favourable wind out to Drangey island. Your companions started throwing stones, trying to hit a certain rock. It was a hot and sunny day, and my son had lain down to rest below that rock because he had been awake all night. You forbade the stone throwing and told the men it was a pointless pastime. They stopped, admittedly, but they mocked your eccentricities and said you had always been a strange one. But if you had not forbidden the game, they would have killed my son."

When the merchant had finished his story, Þórður prepared to leave, for the weather had cleared. He said his farewells to the household, and the merchant accompanied him along the way, wished him a good journey, and they said goodbye. Þórður walked homewards and when he looked back a little while later he saw nothing but Þórðarhöfði nearby. He was most astonished but went on to his home, where he met his wife. He told her the whole story, showed her what he had bought and gave her the shawl. She was delighted by this and thanked him for the gift. Þórður's purchases were put on show and seen by many. Such fine goods had never before been seen in Iceland. Þórður never again saw the merchant or any of his people, but he kept some of the goods he had bought all his life and had them on display.

21. Hálfdan of Fell and the Woman of Málmey

In the outer reaches of Skagafjörður, not far off the eastern shore, there is a small island. This is Málmey, which lies farther out than Drangey; it is about 4 km long and 2.4 km^2 in area. Low-lying at the southern end, the island grows higher to the north, and its highest point, Kaldbakur, rises 156 m above the sea. The view from Kaldbakur in fine weather is said to be unparalleled. The island is green and fertile; it was inhabited for many centuries until 1950, when the farmhouse burned down and the last inhabitants moved away. Málmey has thus had a long and eventful history, including important events during the time of Bishop Guðmundur the Good in the 13th century. Until the 18th century, the island had its own church, served by the pastor of Fell in Sléttuhlíð on the mainland. Various traditions were attached to Málmey; it was forbidden, for instance, to keep horses there, and according to another tradition, if a couple lived on the island for more than 20 years, the wife would vanish, never to be seen again.

Fell in Sléttuhlíð is on the main road from Hofsós along the eastern shore of Skagafjörður. There is no longer a pastor at Fell but the parish church still stands. Many renowned pastors served the parish in former times, some of them known for their supernatural skills. The most famous of these was the Rev. Hálfdan Narfason, who served the parish in the early 1500s. He was said to be a learned man, with great powers of sorcery. One of the best-known tales of the Rev. Hálfdan tells *of the disappearance of the farmer's wife on Málmey, and of her husband's attempts to get her back with the help of the occult arts of the pastor at Fell:*

In the days of Hálfdan, pastor at Fell, a man named Jón lived on Málmey island. He was a married man and wealthy, when this story begins. Jón had begun his farming on Málmey and lived there ever since. Now, however, the twenty years during which his wife was supposed to be safe on Málmey had passed, and nobody dared live there longer. But Jón, being a determined character and sceptical of superstition, decided to stay there, for Málmey was his inheritance. The twenty-first year now passed without event until Christmas. But on Christmas Eve Jón's wife vanished and nobody knew what had become of her, though they searched far and wide.

Farmer Jón was most grieved by this and wanted to find out why his wife had vanished, so he went to see the Rev. Hálfdan at Fell and told him about his problems. The pastor told him that he could indeed find out what had happened to Jón's wife and where she was, but that would be of no use to her husband, as he could not get her back. The farmer asked if he could arrange for him to see his wife, as he felt it would be a comfort to him to know where she was. The pastor said he was most reluctant to do this, but when the farmer repeatedly begged him he agreed to do so. He told the farmer to come to him on a certain day, when everybody had gone to bed.

Farmer Jón arrived at Fell at the agreed time, and found the pastor awake and prepared to travel. A grey horse stood at the northern end of the churchyard, saddled and ready to ride. The pastor went to the horse and mounted. He invited Jón to sit behind him, saying: "But I warn you that you must not speak a single word, whatever happens. If you do, your life is forfeit." The pastor set off, and the farmer was astonished at how fast they travelled. They took the shortest route out to the mouth of the fjord, beyond Dalatá and Siglunes, and headed for Ólafsfjarðarmúli. Once the farmer was alarmed when the horse made a sudden move, and he cried out. "It slipped on a skate: now shut up," said the pastor – and this has been a saying ever since.

No more is said of their journey until they came ashore north of Ólafsfjarðarmúli, where there were great, steep cliffs. They dismounted and the pastor went to the cliff-face. He took a little rod and knocked on the rock. After a short while it opened and two women clad in blue came out, leading farmer Jón's wife between them. She was changed and quite unrecognisable – swollen and bluish, like a troll. The mark of the cross was visible on her forehead, in the true colour of her flesh. The Rev. Hálfdan later said this was the mark of her baptism, the only clue to her former existence. The woman spoke to her husband: "So you're here, Jón. What do you want of me?" The farmer was lost for words and the pastor asked him if he wanted his wife back, or to speak to her. The farmer said no. The pastor then gestured to the women to return to the rock and closed it behind them. He closed the doors in such a way that the women would pose no danger to anyone ever again. Since then, the place where the pastor opened the rock in the north of Ólafsfjarðarmúli has been known as Hálfdanarhurð (Hálfdan's Door). It is red and quite different from the surrounding rock.

The Rev. Hálfdan and the farmer of Málmey went back the way they had come and arrived at Fell before anybody was up. They dismounted in the same place by the northern end of the churchyard and the pastor removed Gráni's harness, accidentally slapping it on the horse's thigh. Gráni did not like this and kicked out at the pastor with his hind leg. The pastor avoided the blow, which landed on the churchyard wall, making a gap. It is said that however often the wall is repaired, the gap always opens up again. It is also said that no one has suffered any harm on Málmey since then, for no one has ever dared live there longer than twenty years.

22. The Deacon of Myrká

The landscape of north Iceland is remarkably diverse, and the spectacular Öxnadalsheiði road over the mountain range between the fjords of Skagafjörður and Eyjafjörður is no exception. This road leads to Öxnadalur, where many of the farms are now uninhabited, as it is a narrow valley between lofty mountains and in winter heavy snow accumulates there. From a cluster of hills that stretches across the valley, a series of spectacular rock pillars rise up high on the mountain ridge to the left. These pillars lie above the farm of Hraun (Lava Field), and are known as Hraundrangar (Lava Pillars). Iceland's favourite romantic poet, Jónas Hallgrímsson, was born at Hraun in 1807.

In a hollow above Hraun is Hraunsvatn (Lava Lake), about 50 m deep. The rock pillars tower above the lake. The largest of them, Hraundrangi, reaches a height of 1,075 m above sea level. Legend claims that up on the rock pillar is a small barrel full of money: whoever finds it first may keep it. No one is known to have scaled the pillar until 1956, when three men reached the top. They found no treasure there, so perhaps someone else had climbed up before, taken the money, and told no one.

Whatever the truth of the legend, the rock pillars are picturesque, and many travellers stop on the road to see this sight. The view down the grassy valley, where the Bægisá river flows into the Öxnadalsá river, is another beautiful prospect. On opposite banks of this fast-flowing tributary stand the farms of Syðri (Southern)-Bægisá and Ytri (Outer)-Bægisá. A church still stands at Ytri-Bægisá. The most *famous of the pastors who served at Bægisá was the Rev. Jón Þorláksson, a poet and translator, whose translations into Icelandic included* Milton's Paradise Lost. *Opposite Ytri-Bægisá, the two valleys of Öxnadalur and Hörgárdalur come together in one broad valley that leads towards Eyjafjörður. In Hörgárdalur is the farm of Myrká (Dark River), formerly a church site with resident pastor. One can hardly pass through this region without recalling a chilling folk tale connected with Myrká and Bægisá:*

Once upon a time there was a deacon at Myrká. He was friendly with Guðrún, a maidservant at the home of the pastor at Bægisá. The deacon came to Bægisá during Advent to invite Guðrún to celebrate Christmas at Myrká. He had a grey-maned horse that he generally rode, called Faxi. It was decided that he would fetch Guðrún on Christmas Eve. Before the deacon rode to Bægisá to invite Guðrún, there had been heavy snow and the rivers were frozen, but on the day he came to Bægisá there was a sudden thaw and the Hörgá river became so swollen and full of ice floes that it was impassable. He left in the evening and crossed the Öxnadalsá river by an ice bridge, but when he reached the Hörgá river, the ice had been swept away. He rode up the riverbank and found an ice bridge. He tried to ride over the bridge but when he reached the middle it gave way and he fell into the river.

The following morning the farmer at Þúfnavellir saw a saddled horse below the homefield and thought he recognised the deacon's mount, Faxi. He was taken aback, for he had seen the deacon cross the river on horseback the previous day but had not seen him return. He walked down by the river and found Faxi there, wet and cold. Then he continued farther down the river and found the deacon dead at the end of Þúfnavallanes. An ice floe had battered the back of his head. The farmer went to Myrká to tell what had happened, and the deacon was transported home and buried in the week before Christmas. No news of this event reached Bægisá, due to the thaw and the state of the rivers.

On Christmas Eve the weather was calm and the rivers were back to normal, so Guðrún looked forward to spending Christmas at Myrká. She started to make herself ready in the afternoon and was almost finished when there was a knock at the door. A woman who was with her went to the door but saw no one. It was neither light nor dark outside, for there were clouds around the moon, so that it was sometimes veiled and sometimes not. When the girl came in and said she could see no one outside, Guðrún said: "This prank is meant for me and I shall go out." She was ready, except that she had not yet put on her coat. She took her coat, put one arm in the sleeve, and flung the other over her shoulder. Outside she saw Faxi and someone she took for the deacon. He took her, lifted her on to the horse and mounted up in front of her. They rode for a while without speaking.

At the Hörgá river the bank was steep and when the horse jumped down, the deacon's hat slipped up at the back. The moon emerged from the clouds and Guðrún saw the bone of his bare skull. Then said the deacon:

Moon glides, death rides;
don't you see the white mark on my nape,
Garún, Garún?*

She was shocked and said nothing. They rode on and no more is reported of their conversation until they reached Myrká, and dismounted by the lychgate, where he said:

Wait here, Garún, Garún,
while I take Faxi, Faxi,
up beyond the churchyard, churchyard.

Then he led the horse away and Guðrún looked into the churchyard, where she saw an open grave. Terrified, she grasped the bell-rope in the lychgate and rang the bell. At that moment she was grabbed from behind. It was fortunate that she had only put one arm into the sleeve of her coat, for she was grabbed so hard that the coat tore at the shoulder seam. Her last glimpse of the deacon was as he tumbled into the open grave with the torn coat and soil swept into the grave from both sides. Meanwhile Guðrún kept ringing the bell, until the household of Myrká came out to fetch her. She was very frightened, for she was sure she had been haunted by the deacon's ghost, even though she had not yet heard of his death. But the Myrká folk soon told her the whole story and she recounted her own journey,

In the evening, when everyone was in bed and the lights had been extinguished, the deacon came back to haunt Guðrún. There was so much noise that it was impossible to sleep. For two weeks she could not be left alone and someone had to sit up with her every night. Even the pastor had to sit with her and read the Psalter. At last, a sorcerer was brought from Skagafjörður in the west. He managed to lay the deacon to rest with a great spell. Finally, he rolled a big rock on top of the grave and there the deacon rests to this day. After this the haunting ceased and Guðrún improved. Soon afterwards she returned to Bægisá but it is said that she was never the same again.

* The ghost cannot speak the name of God (Guð) in Guðrún's name.

23. The Grímsey Man and the Polar Bear

Grímsey island, 41 km offshore, is Iceland's northernmost community, intersected by the Arctic Circle. The island is 5.3 km^2 in area and 105 m above sea level at its highest point. Most of its coast is made up of cliffs, except in the south. The climate of Grímsey is relatively mild and it has considerable vegetation. Many birds nest on the cliffs, where they are hunted and their eggs gathered for food. In the past there were generally 12 farms on Grímsey, sometimes more; the islanders traditionally lived by fishing, farming and harvesting other natural resources, such as seabirds' eggs. Today the island has an excellent harbour and an airstrip, and regular communications with the mainland are maintained by sea and air. In recent years, a growing number of tourists have visited Grímsey, where a special certificate is issued to those who cross the Arctic Circle. The population of the island has fluctuated greatly over the centuries, and it appears to have been uninhabited in some periods. Today the islanders number about 100, and the local economy is based on the fisheries. Grímsey had its own resident pastor in former times and into the 20th century; a church stands at Miðgarðar, which is now served by a pastor from Akureyri. The island also has a shop, postal service, community centre, weather observation station and so on. In the 19th century the Grímsey islanders were known for their skill at chess. A wealthy American, Willard Fiske, heard of this, and visited Iceland. Wanting to do something for the islanders, he gave them chess sets, a collection of books and a fund to buy more books.

Grímsey played an important part in the civil conflicts of the 13th century, especially in the confrontation between Bishop Guðmundur the Good and the magnates of the Sturlung Age. After slaying Tumi Sighvatsson at Hólar in 1222, the bishop's followers fled to Grímsey. Tumi's father Sighvatur and his brother Sturla then sailed out to the island with a force of armed men. A great battle was fought there and many lives were lost. The bishop's men were defeated and Bishop Guðmundur himself was captured and sent to Norway.

Heimskringla, Snorri Sturluson's history of the Kings of Norway, tells how King Olaf Haraldsson coveted Iceland in the early 11th century. When his suggestion to take control of Iceland was rejected by the Althing (Icelandic parliament), the royal representative proposed that Iceland give the king Grímsey as a token of friendship. Many men thought this was a good idea but Einar Þveræingur was of a different view: he opposed giving away any land and pointed out that the king could maintain a whole army on Grímsey and attack the mainland at his pleasure. Convinced by his arguments, the Althing decided against giving the island to the king.

Polar bears have often drifted across from Greenland on sea ice and ambled ashore on Grímsey. One such bear was shot in 1969; it was stuffed and is on display at the Húsavík Natural History Museum. Folklore tells of another bear that visited the island long ago and received a rather warmer welcome:

Once upon a time all the fires had died on Grímsey, so that no fire could be lit on any farm. This was before the days of matches, so the only option was to go to the mainland to fetch embers. At that time the weather was very calm and the frost so severe that Grímsey Sound was frozen over. Three hearty men were sent ashore; they set off early in the morning in clear weather. Nothing is reported of their journey until they reached a gap in the ice. Two of the men jumped across but the third was afraid. The two men went on and told the third to return to the island. He did not like to turn back and so he walked along by the gap, hoping to find a place to cross. As the day went on the sky grew overcast and a southerly wind came, bringing rain and wind. The ice then began to break up and finally the man found himself on an ice floe being carried out to sea. In the evening he reached a tongue of ice and jumped on to it. But as soon as he had reached it he saw a female polar bear with two cubs close by. The man was both cold and hungry, and now he feared for his life. The bear watched the man for a while, then stood up, walked over to him and gestured to him to lie down in her lair. The man did so, although he was apprehensive. Then the bear lay down and allowed the man to suckle her milk, like her cubs.

The night passed. The next morning the bear stood up, walked a short distance from the lair and indicated to the man to follow. Then the bear crouched down and gestured to the man to climb on her back. He did so and the beast then stood up. Then she shook herself so violently that the man fell off. Three days passed. The man slept in the bear's lair and drank her milk, and every day the bear had him climb on her back and shook him until he fell off. On the fourth morning he did better and could cling on no matter how the beast shook him. Later that day, the bear set off swimming with the man on her back and took him home to Grímsey. When they came ashore the man gestured to the beast to follow him. He took her to his home, had his best cow milked and gave her as much milk as she wanted, warm from the udder. Then he took the beast to his sheep-shed. He had his two finest sheep slaughtered, tied them together by the horns and hung them across the bear's back. Then the bear swam out to sea, to return to her cubs with the sheep. The Grímsey folk now had reason to be happy, for as they were watching the bear's departure in amazement, they observed a ship approaching fast from the mainland. Their two messengers had arrived, bringing fire. Now all three men had returned, and the islanders could once again light fires and cook food.

24. *Waterfall of the Gods*

Iceland boasts a multitude of waterfalls of all shapes and sizes. Wide and narrow, high and low, large and small, famous and obscure, their variety is almost inexhaustible. One of the most picturesque and famous waterfalls in Iceland is Goðafoss (Waterfall of the Gods), in the Skjálfandafljót river; most travellers in the north stop to admire it. The waterfall is also conveniently located, just off the Ring Road between Akureyri and Mývatn, at Fosshóll in the Bárðardalur valley.

Akureyri, the main town of north Iceland, stands in a delightful location by the Pollur, the innermost part of Eyjafjörður. From there, the route crosses Leirur by bridge, then passes through Svalbarðsströnd. Along with many farms, the area is said to boast many elf communities in the rocks and cliffs. Tall mountains with snow-capped peaks may be seen to the west. The highest peak is Kerling, 1,538 m, which rises above Grund in Eyjafjarðarsveit. Soon, the road steepens on the Víkurskarð pass to Fnjóskadalur, where the Vaglaskógur woods nestle. Next it crosses the Fnjóská river, just north of the woods, and then the Ljósavatnsskarð pass, with the delightful Ljósavatn lake. To the left is Kaldakinn, while ahead and to the right is Bárðardalur. Through this valley flows the powerful Skjálfandi river, and straight ahead the spray can be seen rising from the historic waterfall, Goðafoss.

Just south of Ljósavatn lake is a very old farm of the same name. Around the year 1000 this was the home of Þorgeir Þorkelsson, chieftain of Ljósavatn, who played a crucial role in Icelandic history. It is to him that Goðafoss owes its name.

Although our tales of Goðafoss are drawn not from folklore but from saga literature, they nevertheless have a strong flavour of folk tradition:

Þorgeir was the Law Speaker at the Althing, who made the fateful decision in AD 1000 that Iceland should become a Christian nation. He himself believed in the old Norse gods when he rode to the Althing that summer, but after the assembly had agreed to his proposal that all Icelanders should be baptised as Christians, he was probably among the first to receive baptism. And so he returned to his home a Christian and had to change all his customs. He set an example by removing all the idols of the Norse gods from his temple, taking them to the Skjálfandi river and flinging them into the water at a great waterfall, which was named after this event and has been known ever since as Goðafoss (Waterfall of the Gods).

The *Saga of Grettir* also tells a story of a waterfall; although the waterfall is not named in the story, it appears to be Goðafoss.

The outlaw Grettir Ásmundarson was hiding out at the farm of Sandhaugar in Bárðardalur. It so happened that during the past two Christmases, the men who were left behind to guard the farm while the rest of the household went to Mass had vanished. First it was the farmer himself, Þorsteinn, who vanished, and the next year a farmhand. Grettir offered to stay home alone and guard the farm on Christmas night. After the people of the household had left, he prepared himself as well as possible, and at first all was quiet. But in the middle of the night he heard a commotion and in came a fearsome troll-wife. She attacked Grettir and they wrestled for a long time, first indoors, then out of doors and far and wide. The troll-wife did her best to haul Grettir down to the river canyon and throw him over the cliffs. She almost succeeded but then Grettir managed to free his right hand and grab his axe. He chopped at her arm, so that it came off and the troll fell into the canyon and the waterfall there. Grettir was exhausted after this struggle but soon recovered, thanks to the good care of Steinvör, the woman of the house at Sandhaugar.

Grettir suspected that there were more trolls in the river canyon. Soon after Christmas he asked Father Steinn of Eyjadalsá to explore the waterfall and its surroundings with him. They thought they could see caves behind the waterfall and Grettir wanted to examine them better, although they were difficult to reach. He took the priest along to look after the rope. After that he prepared for his expedition: he wore few clothes and put his axe in his belt, bearing no other weapon. Then he jumped off the cliff and into the waterfall. The priest saw the soles of his feet, but did not see what became of him. Grettir dived beneath the waterfall, which was difficult due to eddies, and he had to dive down to the bottom before he could come up under the waterfall. There was a rock there, so he could climb up. He saw a huge cave where the river cascaded over the falls. He entered the cave and saw a great fire and a fearsome giant sitting there. When Grettir reached him, the giant jumped to his feet, grabbed a big spear and struck out at him. Grettir struck back with the axe, hitting the spear shaft so that it fell into two pieces. The giant then reached for a sword that hung in the cave. Grettir struck at the giant's breast, so that almost all his chest and belly were cut off and all his guts tumbled into the river. As the priest sat by the rope, he saw the bloody guts carried along by the current. Then he left the rope and ran all the way home. Evening had come and the priest said that Grettir was certainly dead by now.

But Grettir did not give up until the giant was dead. Then he lit a light and went farther into the cave to explore. It is not known how much treasure he found but it is said to have been considerable. He remained there for much of the night. He found the bones of two men and took them with him in a sack. Then he left the cave and returned to the rope and shook it, for he thought the priest was there to pull him up.

When he realised the priest had gone, he had to climb up by his own strength and he reached the cliff. Then he went to Eyjadalsá and put the sack of bones in the vestibule of the church, so that they might later be buried in hallowed ground. After Grettir's feat, trolls and other monsters caused no more harm in Bárðardalur.

25. The Night Troll and her Boat at Mývatn

It is the general consensus that Lake Mývatn and the area around it, with its splendour and variety of landscape and its abundance of natural resources, are one of the Creator's masterpieces. The lake and its environs are also one of Iceland's major tourist attractions, often called by such names as the "jewel of the north".

Lake Mývatn (Midge Lake) derives its name from the clouds of midges that may be seen there on fine days. When the vast numbers of midges fly up in a dark mass, it sometimes seems as if the sun is covered by cloud. Lake Mývatn is 36.5 km^2 in area, and hence Iceland's fourth-largest lake. It is relatively shallow, no more than 4.5 m at its deepest point. The shore of the lake is heavily indented, and there are about 40 islands and islets of different sizes. One of the best known of these is Slútnes, famed for its luxuriant vegetation. Mývatn boasts abundant bird life, including a larger number of duck species than anywhere else on earth. The ducks' nesting colonies were an important resource in times past and duck eggs are still gathered today. The lake also offers better trout fishing than any other Icelandic lake, and the Mývatn trout is reputed to be better and tastier too. The trout in the lake have always been a valued resource; in former times it was said that there was never famine at Mývatn, even though people might be dying of hunger in other regions.

The people of the Mývatn area have fished the lake since time immemorial, and a tale is told of successful fishing there in the 13th century, when Bishop Guðmundur the Good was travelling about the country. Once the bishop arrived at Mývatn, accompanied as usual by a great number of followers. He stayed overnight with all his company at Reykjahlíð, which has long been a calling-place for visitors to the lake, and still is. The farmer was not prepared for such a large number of guests and he ran out of food. Then he resorted to slaughtering three of his cows to feed all the visitors. Bishop Guðmundur was most grateful to the farmer for his hospitality and generosity, and he blessed all the resources of the Reykjahlíð estate. After this the farmer caught so much fish that summer that the catches more than compensated for the value of the three cows. Such good fortune was attendant on playing host to Guðmundur the Good and his followers.

Lake Mývatn and its surroundings are well worth additional consideration: south of the lake rise two great table mountains, Bláfjall and Sellandafjall, and to the southeast is Búrfell. In the east are the mountains Hverfjall and Námafjall, and to the north Krafla, Hlíðarfjall and Vindbelgjarfjall. Large lava fields may be seen east of Lake Mývatn, and bizarre lava formations are found at Dimmuborgir (Dark Fortresses), along the lake at Kálfastrandarvogar and elsewhere. A huge explosion crater on the northwest side of Mt. Krafla, Víti (Hell), formed in an explosive eruption in 1724 – the start of the "Mývatn Fires" which continued for five years. Recent lava fields may be seen around Leirhnjúkur and northwest of Mt. Krafla; these date from the "Krafla Fires" of 1975–84. Hverfjall, like Víti, is an explosion crater, formed about 2,500 years ago. Other important landmarks around the lake include the pseudo-craters at Skútustaðir, the geothermal area at Námaskarð with its sulphur and mud springs, and a delightful garden of trees and flowers that has been cultivated on Höfði, a small headland projecting out into the lake.

East of Lake Mývatn are Lúdentsborgir, a row of craters that derive their name from Lúdent, an explosion crater a little farther east. South of Lúdent is a slope known as Nökkvabrekka (nökkvi is a kind of boat, brekka = slope). A solitary rock on the slope resembles a boat in shape. The story of this boat or nökkvi is recounted in a folk tale:

Long, long ago, a troll-wife lived in the highland above Mývatn, which has been known ever since as Skessuhali (Troll-wife's Ridge). She was a night troll, and they are of such a nature that they must not see the sun, so they do their work by night. The troll-wife did the Mývatn folk great harm, for instance by stealing fish from the lake during the night. She is said to have had a small boat, which she rowed out on the lake, then carried home on her back before dawn.

One summer there were good catches in Strandarvogur bay. This was the best fishing-place in Lake Mývatn, and it has generally been so. The troll-wife made a habit of stealing the fish from the bay every night and the farmer at Strandarvogur was most discontented with this. One night in late summer, the troll-wife made for the bay to go fishing but when she arrived the farmer was there, fishing in her place. She did not feel able to tackle the farmer, for he had another three men with him. So she decided to wait until he had finished fishing.

But the farmer took his time, because he knew what the troll-wife planned to do and so he went on till near morning. The troll-wife was growing impatient but she did not want to give up and leave. When the farmer finally stopped his fishing, the troll-wife went and laid her nets in the bay. When she had finished fishing, she set off for home. But when she was a little more than halfway home to Skessuhali, the sun came up. Then the troll-wife is said to have put down the boat and climbed into it. And both boat and troll-wife turned to stone.

Evidence of the troll-wife's sad demise may still be seen. The boat still stands on Nökkvabrekka, about halfway between Mývatn and Skessuhali. The boat is similar in shape to those that are generally used for fishing on the lake, but larger. Signs of oars and rowlocks are even visible. And a pile of rock in the stern of the boat is believed to be the troll-wife, in her last resting place.

26. Ásbyrgi: Sleipnir's Hoofprint

Beyond the pleasant town of Húsavík on Skjálfandaflói bay, the road continues to the Tjörnes peninsula. Off the shore to the left is the island of Flatey in Skjálfandi. Inhabited in former centuries, the island is now deserted. Off the right-hand shore, Lundey island rises up from the sea, high and bounded by cliffs. The island has never been inhabited but is home to abundant bird life, as indicated by the name Lundey (Puffin Isle).

In the west of Tjörnes there are tall cliffs along much of the shore. In many places, geological history may be seen in the rock strata, going back millions of years in layers of sedimentary rock, shells, lignite, etc. An easy route leads from Hallbjarnarstaðir down to the sea, where remarkable fossil strata may be seen. Farther out on the peninsula are more layers of lignite (brown coal), which was mined for fuel on the estates of Ytri-Tunga and Hringver during World War I, when imported coal was in short supply.

Farther along the peninsula, Grímsey island may be glimpsed far out to sea. Closer to the mainland are the Mánáreyjar islands, two small islands just offshore from the farm of Máná. In 1867 there was an underwater eruption adjacent to the islands. The road continues around the northern end of Tjörnes and heads south along its eastern shore, where there are many tall sea cliffs and splendid views to the east over Öxarfjörður. Across the bay is Melrakkaslétta, the northernmost habitation on Iceland's mainland; two points of land, Rifshafnartangi and Hraunhafnartangi, stretch out northwards to touch the Arctic Circle. The route from the Tjörnes peninsula ends at Auðbjargarstaðabrekka, a steep mountain road. Below the slope is the farm of Auðbjargarstaðir, where Kristján Jónsson, "the Mountain Poet", grew up. This is the district of Kelduhverfi, which stretches from the Tjörnes mountains eastwards to the river Jökulsá á Fjöllum.

The community of Kelduhverfi is comprised of two parts. Some of the farms are located on the estuary of the Jökulsá river, while others stand in ancient lava fields farther south. The area is volcanically active, with frequent tremors. East-west movements in the earth's crust have produced many fissures; a series of earthquakes began in 1975, forming more new fissures and gullies.

The road leads past the farms of Víkingavatn, Lón and finally Keldunes, where Skúli Magnússon, known as the "Father of Reykjavík", was born in 1711. A monument has been erected here in his memory and the community centre is named Skúlagarður in his honour. Farther east, near the Jökulsá river, the entrance of Ásbyrgi (the Gods' Bastion) opens up on the right, like a portal to a fairytale castle. Ásbyrgi is a huge depression in the earth, 3.5 km long and more than one kilometre across, surrounded by near-vertical cliffs 90–100 m high. The entrance is divided in two by a tall rock named Eyjan (The Island). The bottom of Ásbyrgi is almost flat, with abundant vegetation and birch woods. There are also rowan trees and tall willow shrubs in among the birches, along with larches, fir and pine trees, which have been planted in recent decades. And in the south of this natural fortress lies a small lake, Botnstjörn.

The origin and formation of Ásbyrgi have long been disputed by geologists, but the consensus now seems to be that Ásbyrgi was formed in massive floods of the Jökulsá river at the end of the last Ice Age, 8–10,000 years ago, and then again about 3,000 years ago. Following this, the river is believed to have cut itself a new course, flowing into its canyon by the farm of Austaraland. The Jökulsárgljúfur canyon is a world of its own, with a great variety of natural formations: Hljóðaklettar, Vesturdalur, Hólmatungur and Forvaðar. Of the many waterfalls in the river, Dettifoss is the largest.

Dettifoss is 44 m high, the most powerful waterfall in Europe. Other waterfalls in the river include Selfoss, Réttarfoss, Vígabjargafoss and Hafragilsfoss. The Jökulsárgljúfur canyon and its surroundings have been a National Park since 1973.

While scientists claim that Ásbyrgi and Jökulsárgljúfur were formed in a huge flood, there are other theories as to how these formations originated. All these events took place thousands of years before man set foot in Iceland, so no witnesses can be produced to verify them. But there is an old folk tale:

Legend says that once upon a time Óðinn, the highest of the Norse gods, was riding through the heavens. He rode through the air on his eight-legged stallion Sleipnir, among the Northern Lights in a starlit sky. The god was a little careless with the reins, riding high and low, not always looking where he was going, and one time he came a little too close to the earth, so that Sleipnir touched the ground with one of his eight hooves, treading down hard. This tore the surface and the earth collapsed underneath. The hoof-print left by Sleipnir is clearly visible today, and is called Ásbyrgi (the Gods' Bastion).

This old tale may well be deemed as good an explanation of the origins of Ásbyrgi as any other. Certainly, all who visit this place will be touched by its beauty and splendour; the thought may even occur that this magnificent cliff-lined fortress must surely be the work of the gods.

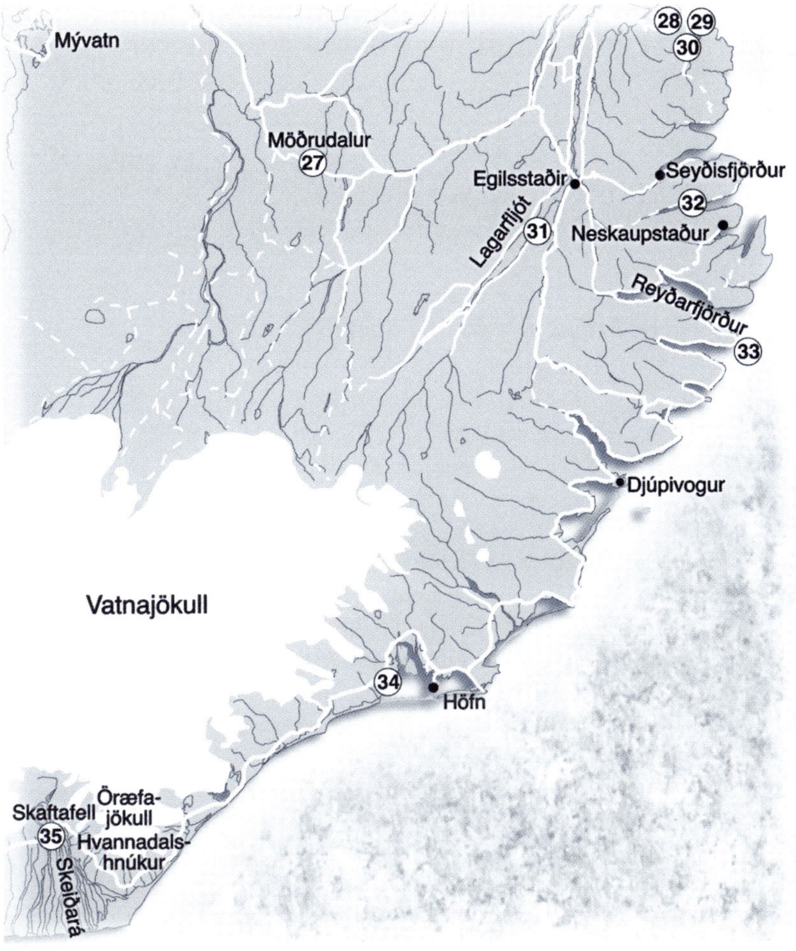

EAST ICELAND

27. Manga of Möðrudalur

From Egilsstaðir, the administrative centre of east Iceland, the Ring Road leads through Fljótsdalur and on to the uplands of Jökuldalsheiði. A number of farms were once to be found on the heath, some of which remained inhabited well into the 20th century. Higher ground begins at Möðrudalsöræfi, and the road north over the Möðrudalur mountain range reaches 660 m above sea level. This road soon reaches Möðrudalur, one of the remotest farms in Iceland. It stands at a higher altitude than any other farm in the country, at 469 m. Möðrudalur was formerly an important manor, and until recently it was a stopping place on the route between north and east Iceland. The uplands around Möðrudalur were once densely vegetated but are now largely barren. In those days this was reputed to be excellent land: the layer of cream on top of the milk vats at Möðrudalur was said to be thick enough to float a horseshoe.

The church at Möðrudalur was built by the resident farmer, a self-taught artist named Jón Stefánsson, who died in 1971. He built the little church, consecrated in 1949, in memory of his wife, Þórunn Vilhjálmsdóttir. He also made all the ornamentation himself, including a painted altarpiece of the Sermon on the Mount. In past centuries there were a number of farms in the region, and the parish church stood at Möðrudalur, which was centrally situated. Möðrudalur also had a resident pastor until 1716, when the farm was abandoned for a time.

The route across the mountains, which formerly passed right through Möðrudalur, has now been moved some distance away. But it *is worth making the short detour to see this historic place, and to recall the story of the pastor's wife, who long, long ago refused to lie still in her grave:*

Bjarni Jónsson was the last pastor of Möðrudalur, and his first wife was named Margrét, known as Manga. She loved the Rev. Bjarni dearly but they did not have a long time together, for she died in childbirth. Prior to her death she asked her husband never to marry again and he gave her his promise. Before she lay on her deathbed, she had been knitting a brown sock of fine yarn. As soon as she was dead, her ghost walked. People heard noises in the larder and kitchen, and she was seen both by clairvoyants and others. She wore a kerchief as in life and was great with child, for she had not given birth, and she was always knitting a brown sock of fine yarn.

Before long, Bjarni remarried. But when the pastor's new wife joined him in bed, Manga appeared and sat in front of him. Then Bjarni said: "Go away, Margrét; the time when you belonged here has passed." The ghost of Manga of Möðrudalur caused a great commotion. She persecuted the Rev. Bjarni's wife and finally brought her to her death. Bjarni then married for the third time. He was advised to marry a woman Margrét had never seen. He brought her from Vopnafjörður and she is said to have outlived her husband.

Bjarni died suddenly one day in early winter on the way between Eiríksstaðir and Hákonarstaðir in Jökuldalur. He was found late in the day and a tent was raised over his body. A courageous young girl from Eiríksstaðir, named Guðrún, was left to guard the body. The tent was close to the Jökulsá river. It was a moonlit night and clouds sometimes veiled the moon. Guðrún recounted that around dusk a great flock of ravens flew up out of the gully by the river. The ravens were grey and they attacked the tent so fiercely that she could not protect it. This continued all night until dawn and all night she saw Manga sitting on the slope above, knitting a brown sock of fine yarn. Guðrún said she had never been so tired as after that night.

After the death of the Rev. Bjarni, the farm of Möðrudalur was abandoned due to the haunting, but the farm buildings remained and occasionally travellers had to seek shelter there overnight. Once the Rev. Gísli Gíslason of Desjarmýri had to seek shelter there, when he was travelling to his parish after being ordained. Night was falling, so he went into the farmhouse at Möðrudalur. He went into the *baðstofa* (living room) and made up a bed on a pallet. There was a high pallet in the *baðstofa*, as well as a pallet at each end. When he lay down and looked around, he saw Manga on the high pallet, knitting. But when he saw her, she rushed downstairs and all night he could hear a great commotion, doors banging and pots crashing, so that he did not sleep a wink.

One day another man sought overnight shelter there. Again Manga sat on her high pallet, knitting. This man was brave and fearless, and he took out his snuffbox and offered her snuff. She was so taken aback that she rushed downstairs and started throwing things around in the larder and kitchen, so the guest could not sleep.

28. Naddi of the Njarðvík Screes

There are many pleasant places to stop along the Ring Road. One of them is Egilsstaðir, a young town that has grown up by the Lagarfljót river. Wooded land rises above the town and the wide river flows below it, while in the distance to the south Mt. Snæfell reaches a height of 1,832 m above sea level.

Turning northward off the Ring Road at Egilsstaðir is a road that crosses the Eyvindará river and continues through the Fljótsdalur district. It then passes through Eiðaþinghá and Hjaltastaðaþinghá and on to the sandy lowlands of Héraðsflói bay. A right turn here crosses the wide, calm Selfljót river, passes Unaós, named for Uni the Dane, son of Garðar Svavarsson (who made one of the first attempts to settle in Iceland, which he named "Garðarshólmi" or "Garðar's Little Island") and up the steep slope to the Vatnsskarð pass. The road over the pass rises to a height of 431 m; at its highest point are a small lake and a mountain hut. This is an excellent spot to pull over and enjoy the view of the splendid Dyrfjöll mountains to the right, with glacial expanses and rugged landscape below.

From here the road descends to Njarðvík, the northernmost bay of the East Fjords. Light-coloured rhyolitic rock is noticeable in the mountains that embrace the valley; farther inland, the land is well vegetated, with some wooded areas. An abandoned farm called Njarðvík stands by the bay. Traces of an old wall, Þorragarður, which is believed to have been built by the Saga-age chieftain Ketill Þrymur, may be seen there.

At the only remaining farm in Njarðvík, Borg, is a place named

Þiðrandaþúfa (Þiðrandi's Tussock), named after a kinsman of Ketill Þrymur called Þiðrandi Geitisson, who was reputed to be the most handsome and virtuous of young men. A Norwegian visitor named Gunnar slew young Þiðrandi more or less by accident, and was known thereafter as "Slayer of Þiðrandi". Þiðrandi's family were keen to avenge his death but Gunnar always managed to evade them. Out in the bay are two skerries where Gunnar is said to have taken refuge, when he fled by swimming from the mainland. In the past there were several farms at Njarðvík and, before the Reformation, there was also a church dedicated to the Virgin Mary, which was served by the pastor of Desjarmýri in Borgarfjörður eystri. That church was formally abolished only a few decades ago and the present church building has never been consecrated.

From Njarðvík the road leads on towards Borgarfjörður eystri, following a steep mountain slope known as Njarðvíkurskriður (Njarðvík Screes). In many places along the route, there are vertical cliffs down to the sea, which have been eroded into hollows and clefts by the action of the waves. The surf makes a great din as it washes into these hollows. In former times the Njarðvík Screes were a fearsome place to travel, where a poor road clung to the steep coastal screes and it was not uncommon for people to lose their lives along the way, not least in avalanches. The most recent deaths were in 1909, when two men perished there. Today, an excellent road along the screes has eliminated much of the risk, though the view remains spectacular.

In the past, the deaths on the Njarðvík Screes were attributed to a creature known as Naddi, reputed to live in a cave in Naddagil (Naddi's Gully), to the north of the screes. Naddi was eventually defeated and after this a wooden cross was raised on the road, bearing a Latin inscription. The cross has been renewed many times and it remains in place today. The inscription reads:

Effigiem Christi,
qui transis,
pronus honora.
Anno MCCCVI.

(Bow down and revere
this effigy of Christ,
you who pass by.
AD 1306.)

Naddi was said to be a monstrous creature, with the upper body of a man and the lower body of a beast. He was rarely seen during the light months of summer but often attacked travellers when the nights began to draw in, and killed many of them.

An old tale tells of Naddi's demise:

One day in late autumn, Jón Bjarnason was on his way home to Njarðvík from Borgarfjörður. Along the way he called at Snotrunes, arriving there at sunset. The people there asked him to spend the night and not to risk the Screes so late in the evening. He said that nothing would happen to him and he continued his journey but when he reached Naddagil, the creature attacked him. There was a great struggle between them, which lasted a long time. They went far and wide in their fighting and eventually came to Krossjaðar, where the creature escaped from Jón and slipped down into the sea. A cross was later erected on that spot, with a Latin inscription saying that travellers should bow down and pray there. After the confrontation with Naddi, Jón reached home at Njarðvík. He was in pain, black and blue with bruises, and he lay in his bed for a month before he was able to get up. But the creature was never seen again after their struggle. Jón believed that it must have come from the sea, since it returned there after being defeated in the fight.

29. The Elf Queen of Snotrunes

Borgarfjörður eystri is the northernmost of the East Fjords, famed for its natural beauty, especially the spectacular Dyrfjöll mountains. A village named Bakkagerði has grown up by the fjord in recent times. Close to the village is a rocky hill known as Álfaborg (Elf Rock), which is said to be one of the major elf communities in Iceland.

From Borgarfjörður, the road leads out to Njarðvík, then over the Vatnsskarð pass to the Fljótsdalur district. The last farm in Borgarfjörður before the infamous Njarðvík Screes is Snotrunes. Once known simply as Nes (Headland), the farm was later named for the elf queen, Snotra, who lived there for a time. The story goes:

Once upon a time a fine lady, whom nobody knew, came to Nes in Borgarfjörður. She settled there and won respect as people came to know her better. Soon she gained control of the entire estate and became the mistress of Nes. She appointed a steward, and challenged him to say where she would be the following Christmas, for she had told him she was going away at that time. She said that he must give the right answer or forfeit his life. If he could answer correctly, she would reward him richly.

Now Christmas was approaching and on Christmas Eve, Snotra – for that was the woman's name – prepared to leave, but nobody knew where she was going. After Christmas she returned, came to the steward and asked if he could say where she had been. He said he could not and after this he vanished, so that no one knew what had become of him. The same happened to the next steward and the third. Each Christmas Snotra went away, and when they could not say where she had been, they vanished. Finally a fourth steward arrived and she made the same demands of him. He said that he would say where she had been at Christmas, if he could.

Now Christmas approached and towards dusk on Christmas Eve Snotra began to make preparations for her departure as usual, while the workers lay down to sleep. The steward, however, stayed awake and observed when Snotra left the house. He followed her and saw that she walked down the homefield to the sea, carrying something under her arm. When she reached the rocks on the shore, she sat down and opened the parcel she was carrying. The steward watched and saw that she took out some light-coloured veils. When she saw the steward she flung one of the veils at him, put another over her head and leapt into the sea. He hastily did the same, followed her and managed to catch hold of one corner of the veil on her back. They went on, as if through smoke or mist, until they arrived in a beautiful land. Snotra walked out of the sea, put her veil in a concealed place and went ashore. He did the same, placed his veil on top of hers and followed her. He saw that the land was fair, with scented herbs and fruit trees, and there were many orchards. Next he saw a most splendid city, with walls around it. When Snotra entered by the city gate, she was met with music by many men and taken by the hand. She gestured to the steward to go to a place where two tall buildings stood. There he found a small building from which it was possible to see in through a window in the large building. He stayed there, and on the first evening he went to the window and saw a great celebration inside. There were bright lights and a multitude of people wearing fine clothes, who danced various dances with music and merriment.

On a throne sat a man of noble mien, and the steward was most surprised to recognise Snotra sitting beside the man, in queenly robes. He stood at the window until the dance was over, the tables cleared and the hall empty. When he was in bed, a young woman brought him food; the same woman always brought him food and drink during his sojourn. Every evening he went to the window and always saw the same: great splendour and entertainment, and the same two people presiding. On the last evening he saw two men come to the man on the throne and they told him that a cow had given birth to two calves, one of which was dead. Two women were supposed to be taking care of the cow, and each blamed the other for the death of the calf. This led to a dispute between the two women, and the chieftain was angered at this news.

When Christmas was over, the steward observed that preparations were made for Snotra to depart once more. A great crowd accompanied her from the hall with music. The chieftain led her from the hall by the hand and sadly parted from her. She returned the way she had come, followed by the steward. They journeyed as if through mist, until they came to land at the same spot from which they had departed. Snotra removed her veil and folded it up. The steward did the same with his and threw it to her. She said nothing and went home. He followed her back to the house and slept until morning. The workers got up as usual and went to their work, and he was the only one left in the house. Then Snotra came to him, wished him good day and asked if he could say where she had been at Christmas. He said he did not know but recited this verse:

Two women disputed the death of a calf;
my lady queen, you know that yourself.
They were too eloquent by half,
furious was the king himself.

"Thank you," said Snotra. "Now you have liberated me from a spell, which took me away from my husband, so that I could never be with him except at Christmas, unless someone could be found to say where I was at Christmas. You were the only one who could do so. For that I give you all my estate and possessions, and you shall enjoy good fortune."

After this, Snotra vanished and was never seen again, but the farm has been called Snotrunes ever since.

30. Borghildur of Álfaborg

Borgarfjörður is one of the most picturesque places in Iceland. Between Njarðvík and Loðmundarfjörður, it is the northernmost of the fjords that cut into the highlands of the East Fjords. About 4 km across and 5 km long, Borgarfjörður stretches from Landsendi in the north to Hafnartangi in the south. In recent times, a village named Bakkagerði has grown up at the head of the fjord. Offshore to the east of the fjord is a small island named Hafnarhólmi, which abounds in seabirds during the nesting season. A harbour wall was built from the shore out to the island, thus providing Borgarfjörður seamen with good shelter for their boats. From the shore, a wide, grassy valley stretches inland, dotted with farms. The valley is surrounded by varied and colourful mountains, where dark basalt and pale rhyolite come together in spectacular rock formations. At the head of the valley the Dyrfjöll mountains rise up, dark and impressive, to more than 1,100 m above sea level. In the lowlands at the village of Bakkagerði stands a rocky hill known as Borg or Álfaborg (Elf Rock). This attractive feature has long been believed to be one of the main centres of Iceland's elf population. Over the years many people have seen these graceful beings. In olden times the elves were believed to attend church in Kækjudalur, a narrow valley inland from Borgarfjörður; in the valley stands a huge rock shaped like a building, which is called Kirkjusteinn (Church Rock). Elves were sometimes seen riding in company to the church in Kækjudalur.

The people of Borgarfjörður eystri live by fishing and fish processing, as well as agriculture. In Bakkagerði there is also a business called

Álfasteinn, where rocks and stones are polished to make jewellery and souvenirs. There is considerable demand for these items, especially as a growing number of visitors make their way to the Borgarfjörður area. The mountains around the fjord are also rich in interesting and attractive stones.

The village of Bakkagerði has a church, school, shop, community centre and so on. In former times the Borgarfjörður parish church stood at Desjarmýri, farther inland, where the pastor resided, but in the early 1900s the church was transported down to Bakkagerði, where the pastor also settled. The church, which is close to Álfaborg, contains an interesting altarpiece painted by Jóhannes Sveinsson Kjarval (1885–1972), one of Iceland's leading 20th-century artists. The altarpiece depicts the Sermon on the Mount; Christ stands upon Álfaborg, with the Dyrfjöll mountains in the background. The altarpiece was controversial when painted, as some deemed it too "worldly" for a church. Though born in the south of Iceland, Kjarval grew up on the farm of Geitavík in Borgarfjörður, and the surroundings of his youth played an important part in his art. And it is possible that the mystical elements of his art reflect the influence of stories of elves and other supernatural creatures that he heard when he was young.

Borgarfjörður eystri is generally acknowledged to be one of the most beautiful regions in Iceland and it is also famed for its rich heritage of folklore; the Borgarfjörður tales of elves or "hidden folk" are unusually imaginative. For example:

Once upon a time a farmer lived at Jökulsá, which is the closest farm to Álfaborg west of the Fjarðará river. He had a maidservant whose name was Guðrún. One Sunday in summer the entire household went to church at Desjarmýri, except the maidservant Guðrún. Her mistress asked her to round up the sheep and milk the ewes. Then she was to skim the milk and churn the butter. The household went off to church and the girl set off to round up the sheep. When she had milked the ewes, she let them out on to the gravel banks below the farm. Then she started to cook dinner and when she had finished her work she went outside to look out for the ewes and take a look around. She saw many people riding along the path below the homefield. They were wearing brightly coloured clothing and rode fine, spirited horses. She was most astonished, for everybody should have left for church earlier. All these people rode by the farm, except for one woman who rode up the homefield to the farmhouse.

The woman was quite elderly, but looked well and had a noble countenance. She greeted the girl and said: "Give me some buttermilk to drink, my girl." Guðrún ran indoors, filled a wooden jug with buttermilk and brought it out to her, and the woman took the jug and drank. When she looked up from the jug, the girl asked: "What is your name?" The woman did not reply, but drank again. The maidservant then asked the same question again. When the woman had drunk from the jug and replaced the lid, the girl saw that she reached into her bodice, took a beautiful linen cloth, placed it over the jug lid and passed it to her as she thanked her. Then the girl asked a third time: "What is your name?" "My name is Borghildur, Miss Curiosity," said the woman as she spurred her horse and rode away from the farm to follow the rest. Guðrún the maidservant watched them; the last thing she saw was that they disappeared behind a grey rock at Kollutungur, which leads to Kækjudalur.

After a long time the people of the household returned from church in the evening. The girl then told them what had happened during the day and showed them the cloth the woman had given her. It was so beautiful that nobody had ever seen such a fine cloth. It is said to have been passed down among Icelandic gentlewomen through the ages. The riders seen by the maidservant were believed to have been elves from Álfaborg, on their way to church in Kækjudalur.

31. The Serpent of Lagarfljót

In east Iceland the Ring Road leads over Breiðdalsheiði heath and down into Skriðdalur, heading for the Fljótsdalur district. The lowlands are green and flourishing, with woods here and there. The centre of this large region is at Egilsstaðir, where a growing town has developed in recent decades. Instead of going straight through the town, however, it is well worth taking a circular detour around the Lagarfljót lake. The road down to the Lagarfljót passes through the Hallormsstaður woods on its way to Fljótsdalur. It is also possible to go around to the other bank of the river, to Valþjófsstaður and Skriðuklaustur, and even to visit the Hengifoss waterfall, before continuing to Fellabær, then crossing the bridge across the broad river to Egilsstaðir.

The Lagarfljót river broadens here to form Iceland's third-largest lake, about 52 km^2 in area, 35 km long and from 1 to 2.5 km across. The lake's most notable statistic, however, is its depth, which is up to 112 m. The surface of the lake lies 22 m above sea level, so at its deepest the lake floor is 90 m below sea level. The lake is always coloured a murky brown by glacial sediment, and in several places natural gases bubble up from the bed, so it rarely freezes in winter. The opaque waters, together with the gases and the great depth of the lake, have tended to lend it an air of mystery, and folk tales have been told of it since time immemorial.

Along the Lagarfljót lake shore are the woods of Hallormsstaður, which cover an area of about 800 hectares; this is Iceland's largest forest. The original woods of Hallormsstaður had sadly declined when the place was first declared a conservation area in 1905, but the trees soon recovered, developing into a fine birch forest. Hallormsstaður has been a centre of afforestation since 1903, and extensive experiments with imported tree species have been conducted there. Today, in addition to native trees, about 50 foreign tree species grow at Hallormsstaður, many of which thrive in Icelandic conditions. The oldest larch grove dates from 1938. A small community has developed in the Hallormsstaður woods in recent decades: in addition to the forestry buildings, there are two schools and several homes. During the summer vacation the schools are converted into a summer hotel, which offers pleasant accommodation for visitors in this wooded spot. Among the places of interest in the woods is the picturesque bay of Atlavík. On the way there, larch woods can be seen growing up outside the traditional bounds of the forest.

According to folklore, a monster lives in the depths of the Lagarfljót. The Lagarfljót Serpent is reputed to have been seen by many people over the centuries. Old annals contain many accounts of this serpent, which was greatly feared. One or more loops of the serpent's body were said to be glimpsed rising out of the water and this was regarded as an evil omen. The serpent never caused any real harm, however, as he was said to have been fettered to the bottom of the lake long ago. In modern times, belief in the serpent has waned, and some maintain that the "monster" was nothing but flotsam and jetsam on the surface of the lake. Yet there are always those who reject such rationalist explanations, and choose to believe that there really is a serpent; after all, the lake is so large and so deep that it may conceal mysteries of which we know nothing. One folk tale of the serpent says:

Once, long ago, a woman lived on a farm in the Hérað district by the Lagarfljót. She had a grown-up daughter, to whom she gave a gold ring. The daughter asked her how she could derive the greatest benefit from the gold, and her mother told her to place the ring beneath a heather-serpent. The girl took a heather-serpent, placed the gold ring beneath it and put them both in her linen chest. The serpent lay there for several days. But when the girl went to check on the chest, the serpent had grown so big that the chest was bursting apart. The girl was frightened, so she took the chest and threw it into the river, serpent and all.

Some time later, people began to see the serpent in the lake, and it started to kill both men and beasts there. Sometimes it also stretched up on to the banks and spewed a horrible poison. People were very concerned about this, but they did not know how to deal with the problem. Finally, two skilled Finns were brought to Iceland. They were commissioned to kill the serpent and fetch the gold.

The Finns jumped into the river but soon returned to the surface. They said the case was hopeless, for the serpent was unbeatable; it was neither possible to kill the serpent nor to get the gold. They also said that another serpent lay under the gold, far fiercer than the first. But they dived down again and again, and finally managed to fetter the serpent in two places: one fetter was behind the flippers, the other in front of the tail. Since then the serpent has been able to kill neither man nor beast, but sometimes it flexes its back up out of the water. When this is seen, it is generally deemed a bad omen.

32. The Troll-wife of Prestagil

Mjóifjörður (Narrow Fjord), one of the numerous East Fjords, cuts into the mainland between Norðfjörður and Seyðisfjörður. It is about 18 km long and about 2 km across in its outer reaches, though narrower farther inland. There is little lowland in the fjord, which is enclosed on both sides by high mountains; the fjord is so narrow that on some farms the sun is not seen for many months during the winter. The tallest of the mountains, Söðull, is 1,127 m high; it stands above the abandoned farm of Fjörður.

A road that is very steep in places leads from Egilsstaður across the mouth of the Fagridalur valley, over the Mjóafjarðarheiði pass and down into Mjóifjörður. At the head of the fjord once stood the manor of Fjörður, which was inhabited into the 20th century; for hundreds of years it had a church and resident pastor, and the churchyard, of the old circular type, may still be seen to the east of the farmhouse site. In the late 18th century, Fjörður ceased to have a resident pastor but the church remained there until 1891, when it was moved down to Brekka, a hamlet that stands farther out by the fjord.

About 100 people once lived in Mjóifjörður, on 10 to 12 farms. In the late 19th century, with the development of herring and cod fisheries and the establishment of a Norwegian-run whaling station, the population rose dramatically, to a maximum of 412 in 1902. But today things have changed; about 30 people now live in Mjóifjörður, most of them in the hamlet of Brekka. It was here that one of Iceland's first ice houses for storing fresh fish was built, in 1894. Below the village is a jetty and some of the villagers still go fishing.

Mjóifjörður boasts considerable vegetation and some low-growing woods, especially in Fjarðardalur, the valley above the fjord. A lighthouse stands at Dalatangi, the outermost point on the northern shore of Mjóifjörður. There has been a lighthouse there since 1899. In former times there were several farms at Dalakálki, inland from Dalatangi, but these have now all been abandoned, like most others in the fjord. The landscape here offers strange and beautiful rock formations, which have no doubt given rise to folk tales such as this one:

Inland from the abandoned farm of Fjörður, in the southern slope of the mountain, is a spectacular gorge named Prestagil (Pastors' Gorge). According to folklore, long ago a powerful troll-wife lived there, who used her magical powers to enchant the pastors of Fjörður, so that she could devour them. She would go to the church when the pastor was in the pulpit and wave her hand rhythmically outside the pulpit window, until the pastor went mad and cried out:

Tear out my guts and my heart,
off to the gorge I'll depart.
Tear out my lust and my seed,
to Mjóifjörður gorge I shall speed.

After this he would run out of the church, into the gorge, and never be seen again.

One day a traveller passed by the gorge. He saw a troll-wife sitting on the cliff top, holding something in her hand. The man asked her what it was and she said she was nibbling at the Rev. Snjóki's skull. The traveller told of what he had seen and this was regarded as bad news.

So it continued for a long time; the pastors of Fjörður vanished, one after the other. This became a problem, for clergymen grew reluctant to serve the parish. Finally, no pastor could be found. Then one clergyman volunteered to go to Fjörður, despite knowing of the creature in the gorge. Before he celebrated Mass there for the first time, he gave instructions as to what should be done if he behaved strangely in the pulpit. Six men were to hurry to hold him still, another six were to go to the church bells and ring them, and ten were to go to the church doors. When this had been decided, the pastor began to say Mass. All went well until he stepped into the pulpit. Then a hand appeared at the pulpit window, waving wildly outside. The pastor went mad and began to chant:

Tear out my guts and my heart,
off to the gorge I'll depart.
Tear out my lust and my seed,
to Mjóifjörður gorge I shall speed.

He made as if to rush out of the church, but then the six men seized him, the other six rang the church bells energetically and ten hurried to the doors. When the troll-wife heard the bells, she ran off. She jumped on the churchyard wall, making a large gap. Then she said: "You shall never stand," and since then the gap in the wall has always opened up again, however well it is repaired. But the troll-wife ran in a panic into the gorge and was never seen again.

The troll-wife is said to have lost the iron shoe off one of her feet when she kicked at the churchyard wall. Hermann Jónsson of Fjörður, who died in 1837, said he remembered this iron shoe, which was used for refuse.

A rock at Prestagil is called Skrúði (Vestments) or Skrúðasteinn (Vestment Rock). The doomed pastors are supposed to have placed their vestments here before they rushed into the gorge to the troll-wife. A rock in the gully is known as Líksöngshamar (Requiem Rock); this is said to be where the pastors howled and screamed as the troll-wife tore them to pieces.

33. The Master of Skrúður and the Pastor's Daughter

The east coast of Iceland is indented with many and varied fjords, known as the East Fjords. The largest of these is Reyðarfjörður, which is 30 km long and fairly wide. It is bounded by the headlands of Krossanes to the north and Vattarnes to the south. Reyðarfjörður features in the very beginning of Iceland's history, for this is believed to be the fjord where the seafarer Naddoður, who had lost his way travelling from Norway to the Faroe Islands, made landfall in the mid ninth century. He is said to have been the first Norseman to come to Iceland; realising that he had landed on a previously unknown island, he called it Snæland (Snowland). He sent some of his men up on to Mt. Reyðarfjall to look for signs of human habitation, such as smoke, but there was nothing to see and Naddoður soon sailed away.

In its inner reaches Reyðarfjörður forks into two on either side of Hólmanes below Mt. Hólmatindur. Eskifjörður extends to the north-west, while the other branch retains the name Reyðarfjörður. At the head of the fjord is a village of the same name, previously known as Búðareyri, while the village in Eskifjörður bears the name of that fjord. From Reyðarfjörður a road leads via Fagridalur to Egilsstaðir; from Eskifjörður a road leads via the Oddsskarð pass and tunnel to the town of Neskaupstaður in the next fjord, Norðfjörður.

At Hólmanes stood the old church of Hólmar, which had a resident pastor. For centuries this was regarded as one of the best benefices in Iceland, due to the excellent resources of the estate and the islands belonging to it. In 1909 the church of Hólmar was transferred to Reyðarfjörður, and in 1930 the pastor's residence was moved to Eskifjörður, so little now remains of Hólmar and its past glories.

A well-known folk tale takes place here. It tells of the disappearance of the pastor's daughter, who was never seen again. According to the story, the girl had been placed under a spell by a troll on the island of Skrúður, known as the Master of Skrúður.

There are many islands off Iceland's east coast but only one, Papey, has ever been inhabited. The islands are renowned for their abundant bird life, however, and some of them, like the island of Skrúður, also play a part in old tales. This rather high, rocky island is located off Reyðarfjörður, close to the mouth of Fáskrúðsfjörður. The island has always belonged to the estate of Vattarnes. It has never been inhabited, except when men visited the island to trap birds and gather eggs. In the past, fishermen also sometimes stayed on the island, in a cave named Skrúðshellir, which is quite large and lofty. Sheep were taken out to the island for grazing and they throve on the grass there. Some animals did not survive, however, and this was generally attributed to the Master of Skrúður, who was said to take the finest sheep. But when the daughter of the pastor of Hólmar vanished, it was a far more serious matter:

Long ago, the pastor's daughter at Hólmar in Reyðarfjörður disappeared. A thorough search was conducted on land and sea, but she was not found. A mountain pillar stands up out of the fjord, called Skrúður. Farmers took their sheep to pasture there in autumn and fetched them after Christmas. Every year, the best sheep vanished, but never any other beast.

One winter a ship rowed out to fish but could not land again, and so took shelter below the cliffs of Skrúður. The crew landed their boat, sat on a ledge of rock on the cliff, cold and wet, and started to chant the *Ballad of the Virgin*. The rock then opened up and a huge man's hand emerged, with a ring on every finger and a scarlet sleeve above. The hand passed out a big dish of porridge, with spoons, and a voice said: "Now my wife is amused. Now I am not amused."

When the seamen were full and refreshed after eating the hot porridge, the dish vanished into the rock. The following day they reached land safely. The "wife" the creature mentioned was believed to be the pastor's lost daughter.

A year later the same events befell another ship. On this occasion the seamen on the rock ledge chanted the *Ballad of Andri*. The same hand emerged, this time with a dish of hot and juicy smoked meat, and a voice was heard from inside: "Now I am amused; now my wife is not amused." The men reached shore, with full stomachs, when the weather settled.

Several years passed, until Bishop Guðmundur the Good (*see p. 77*) was travelling in the east. He blessed lakes and springs, and he bound the serpent under the waterfall in Lagarfljót. He stayed at Hólmar, and the pastor asked him to consecrate Skrúður. The same night the bishop dreamt that a huge man in fine clothing came to him and said: "Do not consecrate Skrúður, for I have much to transport and it is a difficult task; and if you go to my home to harm my people, that will be your last journey." The bishop took note and decided against consecrating Skrúður.

34. The Pastor of Einholt

The view from the *Almannaskarð* pass down over *Austur-Skaftafell* district is spectacular, encompassing the rugged mountainous landscape and the *Vatnajökull* ice-cap, with its many glacial tongues that extend down to the lowlands, such as Hoffellsjökull, Fláajökull, Heinabergsjökull, Skálafellsjökull and Breiðamerkurjökull. To the west of these mighty glacial tongues rises Öræfajökull, an ice-cap whose peak, Hvannadalshnúkur, is the highest point in Iceland at 2,119 m. From the glacier flow many voluminous and fast-flowing rivers, and the area directly south of the glacier consists mainly of expanses of shifting sands interspersed with grassy areas.

Habitation in this area is generally sparse, due to the natural conditions. East of the *Almannaskarð* pass is the Lón district, between the mountains of Eystrahorn and Vestrahorn. West of the pass is Nes, where the regional capital, Höfn, is located on low-lying spits of land between Skarðsfjörður and Hornafjörður. Höfn is a relatively young community; the first building there was constructed in 1897, when the old trading centre at Papós was abandoned and moved to Höfn. Beyond the Hornafjarðarfljót river is the Mýrar region, and beyond the river Kolgríma is Suðursveit. Finally, beyond the Öræfajökull ice-cap, is Öræfasveit. These communities were once cut off from the outside world – and indeed from each other – by the hazardous glacial rivers. But road construction, or more specifically bridge-building, has changed all that. The Jökulsá í Lóni river was bridged in 1952, the Jökulsá river at Breiðamerkursandur in 1967, and finally the Skeiðará river in 1974, which completed the Ring Road around Iceland.

Many tales and legends have been preserved in the communities of the Austur-Skaftafell district. Centuries ago, Einholt in Mýrar had a church and resident pastor. One pastor who served there in the 18th century was subjected to various supernatural trials and tribulations, but he was fortunate enough to have women in his household who knew what to do:

Before he became pastor at Kálfafellsstaður, the Rev. Vigfús Benediktsson served at Einholt. At that time there was a man at Viðborðssel named Ólafur, who quarrelled fiercely with the pastor. One day the pastor intended to go visiting his parishioners. His wife asked if he intended to visit Viðborðssel and he said that he did. She said that in that case she would go with him. The pastor was reluctant, for the weather was bad. So she did not go but said: "Take care that nothing happens, and I advise you not to go to Viðborðssel."

Then the pastor went visiting and came to Viðborðssel sometime after sunset. Ólafur gave him a friendly welcome and invited him indoors. Then he took a bottle from a chest, placed it on the table and offered some to the pastor. The pastor did not drink but after a little while he started loosening the cork. At that moment, the door was flung open and Málfríður, the pastor's wife, rushed in and said: "Fúsi, don't drink from the bottle." She grabbed the bottle, drank and spat the drink out on the floor, and the dog that was in the room licked it up and dropped down dead. Then she said to the pastor: "Now you are safe to drink." He took it and drank, and it did him no harm.

Another time, Vigfús was on a journey and travelled through the Öræfi district. Late in the day he arrived at Hnappavellir; he planned to go on that evening to Hof, which is not far off. He was offered an escort, but he did not think this necessary and set off alone. Late that night or in the early hours of the morning, someone appeared at the window at Litlahof, a croft near Hof. The mistress went out and was surprised to see the pastor out at this time of night.

He asked the woman to allow him to stay the rest of the night and to keep a light burning all the time. Meanwhile, Málfríður, the pastor's wife, lay down at dusk but woke up immediately saying: "Now my Fúsi is in trouble." She took a grey cloth from her bodice and started to gnaw on it. She continued all that evening and all night until it was nearly dawn, when she stopped, saying: "Now I'll leave it. I think he's safe now."

Before the Rev. Vigfús came to the east, he had served the parish of Staður in Aðalvík in the west (*see* p. 48). There were powerful magicians there, especially two brothers who persecuted the pastor. He was said to have left the area for this reason. But these men felt they still had some grudge against the pastor after he left, so they woke up a ghost and sent him east to kill the pastor. This ghost, a man of average height dressed in leather, arrived at Tvísker at dusk on Shrove Tuesday. Everyone was asleep except the farmer, whose name was Einar. He heard the door of the house opening. Then he went outside but saw no one, so he returned inside, locked the door and lay down. But when he had lain for a little while, he heard the door open again and the same thing happened. But the third time, a man dressed in leather came in and this was the ghost sent from the west.

The stranger did not say anything. Then the farmer asked him where he was from and he said he was from the West Fjords. The farmer asked him what news he had and he said that Einar had a dead ewe in the fields. The farmer was suspicious when he heard that the West Fjords man knew the earmark of his sheep, and asked him how he knew the ewe was his, but the stranger made no answer. Then the farmer asked about a key that had been lost for twenty years and the stranger told him where it was, as well as other lost items. Now the farmer felt that the ghost was uncomfortably close to him. So he plucked up courage and said to him: "Get out." The ghost then reluctantly went out, taking all the doorframes with him on his shoulders; they were found in fragments around the field the next day.

The ghost now continued his journey until he reached Einholt. The Rev. Vigfús had a nanny, who knew many things. One evening the old woman had the pastor sleep in her bed, while she lay down in his. In the morning, the bedclothes in the pastor's bed were all ripped to shreds, while the old woman herself lay on the floor, so weak that she could hardly tell of her confrontation with the ghost. But she was able to say that the sorcerer brothers in the west would hardly send any more messengers to the pastor, and with that she died.

35. The Troll-wives of Skaftafell

Continuing west the Ring Road passes through Síða and Fljótshverfi. It is well worth stopping at Núpsstaður, the easternmost farm in the Vestur-Skaftafell district. The landscape is awesome here, with strange rock formations towering above the farm. The chapel at Núpsstaður is small but beautiful, dating from the 17th century, with turf walls and roof, and a wooden gable at the front. Beyond Núpsstaður, the road continues past Lómagnúpur, one of Iceland's most impressive cliff formations, 688 m high. Njál's Saga recounts a dream dreamt by Flosi of Svínafell: he saw a giant emerge from the mountain at Lómagnúpur with an iron staff in his hand and call out the names of all those who participated in the burning of Njáll and his family at Bergþórshvoll.

The road continues across Skeiðarársandur, the shifting sands below the glacier. Trusty bridges cross the rivers of Núpsvötn and Sandgýgjukvísl. To one side is the Skeiðarárjökull glacier, wide and flat, while to the other is the North Atlantic Ocean. Straight ahead, the Öræfajökull ice-cap rises up, with its glacial tongues extending down into the lowlands: Skaftafellsjökull and Svínafellsjökull, with sharp-edged Hafrafell between them. To the left, the mountain Þumall (Thumb) stands out from the Skaftafell mountains and the peaks of Kristínartindar jut up from Skaftafellsheiði, while straight ahead is Hvannadalshnúkur, Iceland's highest peak at 2,119 m. To the left, between two valleys, lies Skaftafell. This was an important manor for centuries, but since 1966 it has been a national park.

The bridge across the Skeiðará river is Iceland's longest, at 904 m. A left turn leads to the Skaftafell service centre. The park rangers have their facilities here and the centre includes a shop and restaurant. There is also a campsite, where vegetation has been established on the formerly barren sands. Excellent footpaths lead from the service centre up into the woods. They pass two gullies, where fast-flowing streams plummet over waterfalls such as Heygötufoss, Þjófafoss and Hundafoss. The most beautiful of the waterfalls is Svartifoss (Black Falls), where the river cascades over a natural "vault" of columnar basalt. After this, the paths continue over Skaftafellsheiði to Sjónasker, which commands splendid views of mountain and glacier, streams and huge glacial rivers, wildflowers and birch woods, ocean and barren sand. Few places include such extraordinary contrasts in natural beauty.

It is well worth taking a walk over to the Morsárdalur valley. Beyond it is the Bæjarstaðarskógur wood, where the birch trees flourish particularly well. The Morsárjökull glacier tumbles down at the head of the valley, giving rise to the fast-flowing Morsá river.

Tradition says that long ago the glaciers were much smaller than they are today, and that there was once a route that passed across the highlands through the middle of the Vatnajökull glacier. The farmer of Möðrudalur, north of the glacier, 170 km away as the crow flies but twice as far by road nowadays, is said to have had rights to cut trees at Skaftafell, while the farmer at Skaftafell had the right to graze horses at Möðrudalur. The shepherd at Möðrudalur was supposed to have his own bed at Skaftafell, and the Skaftafell shepherd at Möðrudalur, indicating that there was once frequent contact between the two farms.

Many renowned men have lived at Skaftafell, including a father and son in the 18th century who were famed for their scholarship and craftsmanship. They made guns, for instance, which were used to shoot seals and polar bears. They are also said to have made a four-wheeled vehicle with sails. They found many materials for their crafts on the shore, among debris washed up from shipwrecked vessels on Skeiðarársandur. The so-called gold ship Het Wapen van Amsterdam, a vessel sailing from India that ran aground in 1667, is reputed to have provided plenty of materials. The skill and knowledge of such men often gives rise to folk tales, suggesting that their skills were not entirely of this world; some of the Skaftafell farmers were supposed to be familiar with the troll-wives of the Skaftafell mountains:

Long ago there was a farmer at Skaftafell named Bjarni, who was an excellent craftsman. A troll-wife lived in a cave above the Skaftafell Woods. She was friendly towards Bjarni; she guarded his sheep in the mountains and his driftwood on the shore. One winter she said to Bjarni that a ship had run aground on the shore. All the men aboard were dead but one. The only survivor was a fearsome savage who would destroy all the south of Iceland unless he were slain. Then she took up an axe and went with Bjarni to the shore, where she did battle with the savage and slew him. This troll-wife lived for many human lifetimes and was amicably disposed towards Bjarni's descendants. Her cave is said to exist today, with a window in the middle of the roof-ridge. The troll-wife's bed is reputed to be cut into the rock, eight ells in length and two ells across [one ell is about 50 cm]. Bjarni is said to have built the cave door and all the door fittings, so that the troll-wife would be comfortable there.

Einar was a renowned man who lived at Skaftafell in Öræfi. He is said to have known a certain troll-wife. Once, when Einar was travelling, he suddenly found himself in thick fog. He suspected that the fog was not entirely natural but made to lead him astray. So he took an axe that he had brought with him and threw it away. The fog immediately lifted and Einar continued his journey, reaching home safe and sound. Just after this, one of his horses collapsed. He found the axe, covered with blood, on a sill outside his farmhouse.

The following year, Einar was travelling and had to cross the Skeiðará river. Before he set off to ford the river, he saw a very large woman coming towards him. When they met she asked him for the loan of his horse to cross the river. Einar was reluctant; he said he was afraid she would overstrain the horse as she did last year. The troll-wife said that she had good reason for doing so, as Einar had played a prank on her. She said that when he threw his axe away it had struck her between the breasts and she showed him the scar it had left. Einar saw that she was telling the truth and he permitted her to ride a horse he was leading. They set off across the river and crossed safely.

It is said that the troll-wife teased Einar and that he said he wished to seek her out to be revenged. He went home and made a copper gun, which still exists at Skaftafell. A little later he went to find her. The troll-wife then made her peace with him and promised to do as he wished. Einar's only demand was that she ensure against anyone stealing timber from his woods beyond the Morsá river.

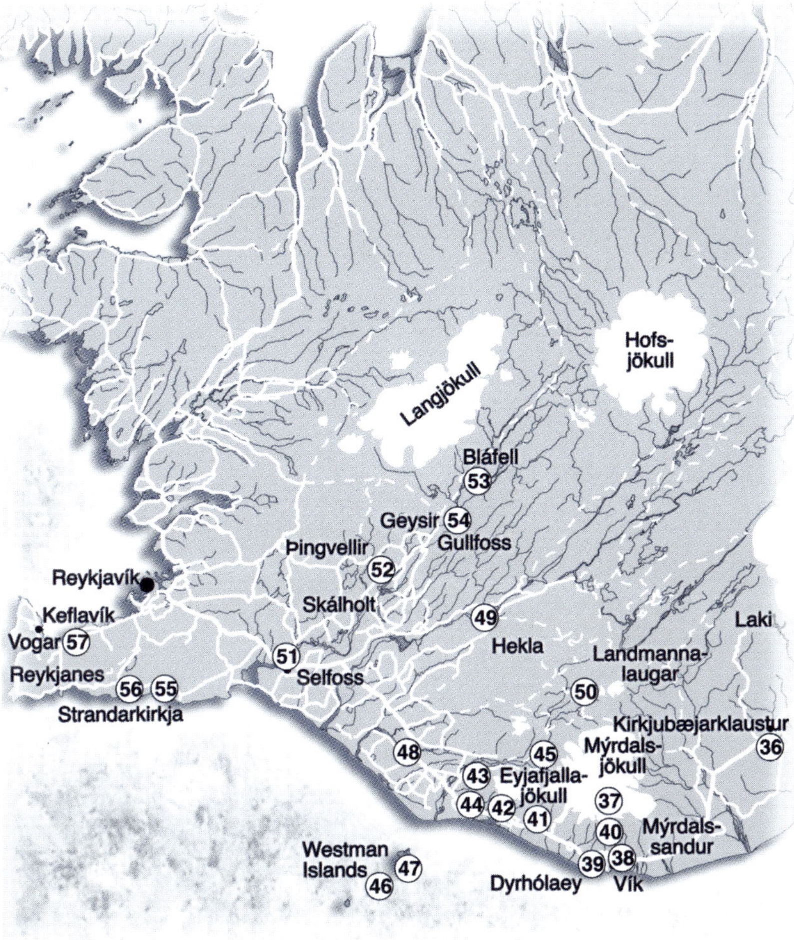

SOUTH ICELAND

36. The Fire Mass at Kirkjubæjarklaustur

Kirkjubæjarklaustur in the Síða district is a beautiful and popular tourist destination, about 270 km from Reykjavík. In former times Kirkjubæjarklaustur was the home of prosperous farmers, district commissioners and regional leaders; in recent years a small village has grown up there, providing various services for the surrounding rural area and for tourists. The village has a shop, hotel/restaurant, post office, bank, school, health-care centre and so forth. In former times it was called Kirkjubær (Church Farm) and, according to tradition, papar (Irish monks) lived here before the Norse settlement in the late ninth century. Kirkjugólf (Church Floor) is an interesting rock formation adjacent to the old farm, where columnar basalt resembles a tiled floor. Legend claimed that this was the floor of a church in the days of the papar. The first Nordic inhabitant of Kirkjubær was Ketill fíflski, who was a Christian, and the belief soon arose that only Christians could live there. After Ketill's time, a pagan named Hildir Eysteinsson planned to settle at Kirkjubær, but fell down dead on arrival there and was buried in the pagan manner at Hildishaugur (Hildir's Barrow). Whatever the truth of the stories of the papar and their church, there certainly was a church at Kirkjubær from early times until 1859, when the church was moved to Prestsbakki. After this, Kirkjubæjarklaustur had no church until 1974, when a chapel was built in memory of the Rev. Jón Steingrímsson (see below).

A convent was founded at Kirkjubær in 1186, which existed until the Reformation in 1550. The name of the place thus changed from Kirkjubær (Church Farm) to Kirkjubæjarklaustur (Church Farm

Convent). Traces of the old convent buildings are still visible at Kirkjuhólar. Several local place-names make reference to the nuns of the convent, such as Systrastapi (Sisters' Rock), Systrafoss (Sisters' Falls) and Systravatn (Sisters' Lake).

Once upon a time, two nuns were up by Systravatn lake. A golden comb was suddenly held up out of the water. One nun coveted the comb, and waded out and drowned. The other took a stone-grey horse that she saw on the bank and rode out into the lake. And neither the nuns, the golden comb nor the horse were ever seen again.

A short distance up the Skaftá river stands an isolated rock named Systrastapi. Two nuns are said to have been burned at the stake upon this rock for violating the moral rules of the convent and for godless behaviour. One sold herself to the Devil, carried consecrated bread by the door of the privy and lay with men, while the other spoke disrespectfully of the Pope. The unfortunate nuns were buried. On one grave grew the most beautiful plants, while few or no plants grew on the other. This was deemed to indicate that one of the nuns had been unjustly condemned.

While there was a convent at Kirkjubær there was a monastery at Þykkvibær in Álftaver, some way south towards the coast. The abbot and his monks of Þykkvibær sometimes went to visit the abbess and nuns at Kirkjubær. These meetings were reputed to be something less than seemly. In those days there was a bridge over the Skaftá river. South of the bridge was a hill where the monks sang to let the nuns know that they were coming; this has been known since as Sönghóll (Song Hill). When the singing was heard, the abbess had the bells rung, and the nuns strode out to meet the guests.

On Whit Sunday, 8 June 1783, a huge volcanic eruption began at Lakagígar, west of the Vatnajökull glacier. The eruption produced a massive lava flow in two places in the lowlands. This is called Skaftáreldhraun (the Skaftá Fire Lava

Field). It extends over an area of 565 km^2 and is the largest flow of lava from a single eruption in history.

Many farms were damaged or laid waste in the disastrous eruption. Toxic gases from the volcano led to deaths of livestock and the haze of gases in the air blocked out the sun, leading to the worst famine in Icelandic history, known as the "Haze Famine".

At one time it appeared that the lava flowing down the Skaftá river might destroy Kirkjubæjarklaustur. The pastor, Jón Steingrímsson, did his best to help his parishioners. As the lava flowed towards Kirkjubæjarklaustur he called them together in the church on Sunday, 20 July 1783. He fervently prayed to God to be merciful and halt the lava flow.

When the congregation came out of the church after this "Fire Mass", they were relieved to see that the lava flow had stopped. This was regarded as a miracle, and the Rev. Jón was dubbed the "Fire Pastor". The place where the lava halted is called Eldmessutangi (Fire Mass Tongue).

The Rev. Jón Steingrímsson (1728–1791) was buried in the churchyard at Kirkjubæjarklaustur, where his grave is marked with a pentagonal pillar of basalt. He is not only known for his bravery during the eruption but was also the author of important writings about that time of suffering. Hence he well deserved the memorial chapel built in his honour at Kirkjubæjarklaustur.

37. Katla of Kötlugjá

East of Vík í Mýrdal the Ring Road passes through impressive landscape, with cliffs on one side and the North Atlantic Ocean on the other. The road soon passes the old manor of Höfðabrekka and Skiphellir (Ship Cave), which was a fishing station until the 17th century. Eruptions of Mt. Katla, which is covered by the Mýrdalsjökull ice-cap, caused huge floods that left massive deposits of alluvium, so that dry land formed where the sea had been. Beyond the cliffs the road crosses Múlakvísl, a fast-flowing glacial river, and sets out across Mýrdalssandur. This sand desert is about 700 km^2 in area, largely barren, with the exception of a small section in the east. To the north rises the Mýrdalsjökull glacier, with a white cap, but fissured and dark with sand on its lower slopes. There is little to catch the eye here, although the Hjörleifshöfði headland may be seen to the south and Mt. Hafursey ahead on the left.

According to medieval sources, this region used to be very different, with vegetation, woodlands and considerable habitation. Place-names such as Dynskógar (Noisy Woods) and Laufskáli (Leafy Bower) are evidence of this. The landscape was entirely different: a fjord once cut into the land by Hjörleifshöfði but has long since become filled up with sand. The farm of Hjörleifshöfði stood for centuries in verdant country west of the headland, until it was laid waste in an eruption of Mt. Katla in the early 18th century. Some time later a new farmhouse was built, but this time up on the actual headland; this was inhabited into the 20th century.

The volcano Katla lies beneath the ice of the Mýrdalsjökull glacier.

This powerful volcano has erupted every 40 to 80 years throughout Iceland's history. Reliable information is available on 16 eruptions but there have probably been more. When Iceland was first settled around AD 900, Katla appears to have been dormant for a long time, since the region had plenty of vegetated, fertile land. So settlers naturally made their homes here, where nothing now remains but barren desert.

A major eruption of Katla soon took place, destroying six farms on the strip of land between the Skálm and Hólmsá rivers. In 1311 another massive eruption took place, known as Sturluhlaup, destroying farms in the Lágey district and killing all its inhabitants except for a young farmer named Sturla and his child. He was on his way home when he saw the glacial flood bearing down on him. His small child stood at the door when he arrived and he picked the child up. At that moment the flood struck and Sturla jumped up onto an ice floe that floated past. He was carried out to sea on the ice floe and drifted for a long time, until the floe was carried ashore or, as some say, fishermen saved Sturla and the child. This is an old tale of a glacial flood from Mt. Katla, which has caused enormous destruction over the centuries. The last major eruption of Mt. Katla took place in 1918, though smaller floods were experienced in 1955 and 1979, without any actual eruption.

In spite of the Katla eruptions, habitation never died out completely on Mýrdalssandur; Álftaver survived, like an oasis in the desert, with several farms and good land. This remote community survived the glacial floods thanks to a cluster of hills north of the district, which diverted the floodwater. The district did suffer some damage, however, as it is believed to have been much larger in the past.

In pre-Reformation times there was a monastery at Þykkvibær in Álftaver. The first abbot there was Þorlákur Þórhallsson (d. 1193), subsequently bishop of Skálholt, who was canonised (though only in Iceland) soon after his death. St. Þorlákur's Day is still celebrated on 23 December.

Many other renowned men were monks at Þykkvibær, such as Eysteinn Ásgrímsson, author of the devotional hymn Lilja (Lily), which has remained popular since the Middle Ages. A folk tale tells of a less than pleasant housekeeper at the monastery:

Once at Þykkvibær, after the monastery was established, the abbot employed a cook whose name was Katla. She had supernatural skills, and she owned a pair of breeches of such a nature that anyone who wore them could run without ever growing tired. Katla used these breeches from time to time. Many people were fearful of her character and her supernatural powers, even the abbot himself. There was also a shepherd on the estate, named Barði. He was often scolded harshly by Katla if any sheep were missing when he rounded them up.

Once the abbot went to a banquet with the cook. Barði was supposed to have brought the sheep home before they returned but he could not find them all. So he put on Katla's breeches, ran as fast as he could and found the sheep. When Katla returned, she realised Barði had used her breeches. She was furious, so she secretly seized Barði and drowned him in a barrel of whey that stood, by old custom, at the main doorway for people to drink from. She left him lying in the whey. Nobody else knew what had become of the shepherd but as the winter passed and the level of whey dropped in the barrel, Katla was heard muttering to herself: "Soon Barði will appear; soon Barði will appear." And when so little was left in the barrel that Katla saw that her wickedness would soon be revealed and she could expect a severe punishment, she put on her breeches and ran out of the monastery and northwest to the glacier, where she was believed to have flung herself into a gully, as she was never seen again.

Soon after that there was a flood from the glacier, heading for Álftaver and the monastery at Þykkvibær. It came to be believed that this eruption and flood were due to Katla's supernatural powers. The gully in the glacier was named Kötlugjá (Katla's Gully) and the land that was laid waste was called Kötlusandur (Katla's Sands), though it is known by most people as Mýrdalssandur today.

38. Jóka of Höfðabrekka and the Pastor of Hörgsland

The Ring Road passes through Vík í Mýrdal, a picturesque town beneath the steep slopes of Mt. Reynisfjall, and continues eastwards by Víkurhamrar, crossing the Kerlingadalsá river to where Höfðabrekka lies a short distance off the road to the left. Höfðabrekka is a good place to stop before setting off across the barren desert of Mýrdalssandur, and various services are available there for travellers.

Höfðabrekka is a large old estate, which was often the home of pastors and district commissioners. In the 17th century a clan of great influence lived at Höfðabrekka; it has been argued that this clan owned a famous manuscript of the Poetic Edda, known as the Codex Regius, which was later sent to Copenhagen and ultimately returned to Iceland in 1971, along with the priceless Flatey Book.

There was a church at Höfðabrekka from the early centuries of Christianity in Iceland until 1929. In pre-Reformation times the church was dedicated to St. Olaf Haraldsson, King of Norway. In former times the farmhouse and church stood on the lowlands below the Höfðabrekkuhamrar cliffs, but in 1660 a large eruption of Katla took place and a massive flood swept westwards along the cliffs. The farmhouse of Höfðabrekka was destroyed but before long the farm was rebuilt on the heath above the cliffs. The farm stood there until 1964, when it was moved down again to the lowlands below Höfðabrekkuháls, where it stands today, just west of Skiphellir cave. The glacial flood of 1660 deposited so much alluvium that the coast-

line moved out a considerable distance. It is said that where there had been 20 fathoms of water in the morning, there was dry land by the evening. Höfðabrekka was formerly known for a notorious ghost, Jóka of Höfðabrekka, who was supposed to have been mistress there.

Long ago, a woman named Jórunn lived at Höfðabrekka. She was a woman of violent temper and harsh character, but other than this she did not have a bad reputation. She had a grown-up daughter, who was a promising woman.

Also at Höfðabrekka lived a man named Þorsteinn, a good man of excellent character. He fell in love with Jórunn's daughter, but she did not like this, and some say that she wanted him for herself but Þorsteinn thought she was too old. Now it happened that Þorsteinn fathered a child on Jórunn's daughter. Jórunn was very angry and said that they should never marry. Many people spoke in Þorsteinn's favour but this only made things worse. Finally, it was agreed that Þorsteinn should go away from Höfðabrekka and have no more to do with the mother of his child.

At Höfðabrekka, the beasts were taken to summer pasture, where they were milked and dairy products were made, and Jórunn's daughter normally went along as housekeeper for the workers. Þorsteinn could not forget the mother of his child, and he seized the opportunity to visit her secretly at the summer pastures and bring her gifts. Jórunn received an exaggerated account of this. She was so irate that she said she would be revenged on Þorsteinn after death, if not in life, and this brought her to her grave. Magnús Pétursson was pastor at Hörgsland at that time and he was regarded as having many supernatural skills. Þorsteinn consulted him and the pastor advised him to go immediately to the Westman Islands. He provided him with an escort all the way and told him not to come back to the mainland for twenty years.

Now the story returns to Jórunn; though she died, her ghost was restless. She was seen doing housework at Höfðabrekka and she was often in the larder serving food but she usually added dirt to it. Otherwise she did no harm to anyone but she walked around with her headdress dangling between her shoulders, which made her look different from other women. She was known by the diminutive of her name: "Jóka."

People often thought they saw her, in various places. Once she met the Rev. Magnús on the road and leant on one of his horses. The pastor said to her: "You did yourself harm, Jóka." But she answered: "Say naught of that, Pastor Mangi. Once you're dead, it's too late to repent." At that moment she vanished but the horse she had leant on had its shoulder broken.

Once two girls stayed up at night in a cowshed. They had a light, and were up on the wooden platform. One said; "How do you think we would react, if Jóka of Höfðabrekka came to us?" At that very moment, Jóka's head appeared over the edge of the platform and she placed her hand on it. She said: "How do you suppose you would react?" She stood there for a while, then vanished, without doing the girls any harm.

Once a ship went out to the Westman Islands, as usual. When the skipper was about to call for the boat to be launched from land, one of the crew said to him: "Are you planning on taking the Devil out to the Islands?" The skipper said he wasn't and asked the crewman what he meant. The man replied that Jóka was on her way out to sea with them. But when this was said, Jóka left the ship; on this occasion no one had seen her but that one man.

When Þorsteinn had been in the Westman Islands for nineteen years, he had had enough and went to the mainland in the spring. This was the time of year when people were flocking to the Westman Islands; among them was the above-mentioned Rev. Magnús. But as soon as Þorsteinn stepped ashore on the mainland, Jóka was there. She grabbed Þorsteinn and tore him to pieces. Just as she finished that task, the Rev. Magnús arrived and Jóka said: "You're late, though you rode hard." The pastor replied: "That's true, but now I intend to see the end of you." The pastor then started to exchange verses with Jóka and his verses were not very polite. One of them was as follows:

Hekla's split is a hellish pit
where raging infernos spit;
I'll show you the door to that great floor,
there's no place that you merit more.

Before long, Jóka vanished, never to be seen again.

39. The Church-builder of Reynir

The Ring Road leads eastward to Mýrdalur, a region of south Iceland that is relatively mild in climate but correspondingly rainy. The route crosses the Jökulsá river on Sólheimasandur, also known as Fúlilækur (Foul Brook), due to its odour of sulphur from geothermal sources upstream. In the past, the river claimed many lives, but in 1921 it was bridged. On the left, the Sólheimajökull glacier slides down to the lowlands and beyond it is Mýrdalsjökull, Iceland's fourth-largest glacier. On the right, a sandy desert leads down to the sea, where the ocean waves beat on the shore. Ahead are the Mýrdalsfjöll mountains and Pétursey, a solitary hill rising to 275 m. South of Pétursey is Eyjarhóll, shaped like a pyramid. These are both said to be the homes of elves. The westernmost farms in Mýrdalur are clustered together at Sólheimar. The first resident at Sólheimar was a certain Loðmundur, in the Age of Settlement; he was said to have supernatural powers. According to the Book of Settlements he feuded with Þrasi at Skógar, west of the Jökulsá river (see page 155). From Sólheimar, a rough track leads up to the Mýrdalsjökull glacier, where snowmobile trips are offered.

Before long, the road passes the Skeiðflöt church. To the right is a turning that leads to Dyrhólaey, a rocky headland at Iceland's southernmost point that rises to 120 m. There has been a lighthouse on the headland since 1910, rebuilt in 1927. Tóin, a point extending to the south from Dyrhólaey, has a hole through the middle, forming a huge natural arch.

Since 1978, when Dyrhólaey became a conservation site, vegetation and bird life have flourished there.

Beyond Dyrhólaey the main road continues up the steep Gatnabrún and through the hills north of Reynisfjall, just above the village of Vík í Mýrdal. At a crossroads, there is a left turning which leads into Heiðardalur, with a picturesque lake and two farms, while the right turning leads to Reynishverfi. South of Mt. Reynisfjall, just offshore, stands a row of rock pillars, Reynisdrangar, the tallest of which is 66 m high. These are no ordinary rock pillars but trolls who were caught in the rays of the morning sun and turned to stone.

The road continues to Garðar, the southernmost farm in Iceland. Below the mountains, by the sea, are bizarre and beautiful formations of columnar basalt in caves at the bottom of the cliff. Bird life is also abundant, especially puffins and fulmars. On the nearby abandoned farm of Hellur are several man-made "caves", one of which used to be lived in. This was the home of the Rev. Jón Steingrímsson, who later became famous as the "Fire Pastor" when he saved the people of Kirkjubæjarklaustur from a volcanic eruption (see page 140).

On the way back from Garðar the road passes Reynir, which was first settled by a certain Björn, a wealthy man. There has been a church at Reynir for many centuries. There was also once a fishing station on the coast nearby, called Reynishöfn. The region boasts considerable natural resources that were highly valued in former times, such as trout rivers, fulmar and puffin colonies, and quantities of driftwood on the shore – a valuable resource in a near-treeless country.

New churches have to be built from time to time, as the old ones become dilapidated just like other buildings. Not much is known of the construction of churches at Reynir, except on one occasion, when an elf named Finnur built a new church in record time. The folk tale is as follows:

Once upon a time a certain farmer lived at Reynir in Mýrdalur. He was to build a church there but he was short of timber for the structure. Haymaking season had arrived, so he had no builders for the work, and he feared that the church would not be completed before winter. One day he was wandering in the fields in a dismal mood, when a man came to him and offered to build the church for him. In return, the farmer was to say what his name was before the construction was completed; otherwise, the farmer must hand over his only son, who was six years old. They agreed on these terms and the stranger set to work. The man paid no attention to anything but his work and hardly said a word, and indeed he worked with astonishing speed. The farmer saw that the church would be completed by about the end of haymaking. Now he grew very unhappy but could do nothing about it. In the autumn, when the church was almost finished, the farmer strolled out beyond the home-field and lay down by a hillock. Then he heard a chanting inside the hillock, as if a mother were chanting to her child:

Finnur soon will come,
your father from Reynir,
to fetch his darling son.

This was chanted over and over again, and the farmer memorised the verse. Now far more cheerful, he walked back to the church. The builder had finished planing the last plank which was to go above the altar and was about to fix it in place. The farmer came to the doorway and said: "So you're almost done, Finnur." The man was so taken aback that he dropped the plank and vanished; he has never been seen again.

40. The Woman and the Sealskin

Mýrdalur is the region between Jökulsá on Sólheimasandur in the west and the Mýrdalssandur desert in the east. This is Iceland's southernmost region, a fertile and well-vegetated area in the shelter of the Mýrdalsjökull glacier.

The Ring Road passes through Mýrdalur and most travellers stop in Vík í Mýrdal, an attractive village located near the sea on lowland below Mt. Reynisfjall. Vík was initially a fishing station but a village began to grow up there after it received its trading charter in 1887. The population is now nearly 400. The local economy is largely based on commerce, light industry and services, not least tourism. The village has a restaurant and guesthouse, campsite and other tourist facilities, and various activities are offered, such as trips by amphibious vehicle out to Reynisdrangar or Dyrhólaey.

The landscape of Mýrdalur is picturesque, with splendid mountains such as Búrfell, Fellsfjall, Pétursey and Arnarstakksheiði inland, and Dyrhólaey and Reynisfjall on the seaward side. In spite of their names, neither Pétursey (Pétur's Island) nor Dyrhólaey (Door-Hill Island) is actually an island. Pétursey is a hill that rises up from the lowlands some distance from the sea, while Dyrhólaey is a rocky headland, 120 m high, with a lighthouse on top. A hole through Tóin, a point extending from the headland, is the "door" of Dyrhólaey. There are many rock pillars at Dyrhólaey: Arnardrangur stands on the shore, while out at sea is Háidrangur, 56 m high. Farther east is Mt. Reynisfjall, 340 m high, and south of this the Reynisdrangar rock pillars rise up out of the sea, the highest reaching 66 m. These pillars *came into existence when two night trolls went to tow a three-masted vessel ashore. They took longer than they expected and were caught in the rays of the rising sun, and so they and their ship were turned to stone. Each pillar has its own name: Landdrangur, Langsamur, Skessudrangur, etc.*

In the past, Mýrdalur had a number of fishing stations: Þórshöfn east of Reynisfjall and Reynishöfn to the west, Dyrhólahöfn at Dyrhólaey, and Maríuhlið on the Jökulsá river. Seals are often seen swimming offshore at Mýrdalur. According to folklore, seals came into existence when the waters of the Red Sea were parted for the children of Israel so that they could pass safely over to the other side; when Pharaoh's warriors followed them, the sea closed over them and they were turned into seals. God mercifully allows them to come ashore once a year, shed their sealskin and make merry in human form until morning. The folk tale of the woman and the sealskin from Mýrdalur suggests that such things really happened:

Once upon a time a man in Mýrdalur was walking by the cliffs along the shore in the early morning, before anybody else was awake. He came to the mouth of a cave and inside the cave he could hear merriment and dancing, while outside lay many sealskins. He picked one up, took it home, and locked it up in a chest. Later that day the man passed by the same place. A pretty young woman sat outside the cave, stark naked and weeping bitterly. She was the seal whose skin the man had taken that morning. He gave her clothes, comforted her and took her home. She was submissive to the man but was reserved with others and often sat looking out to sea.

After a while they were married. They were happy together and had seven children. The farmer always kept the sealskin locked in the chest and carried the key with him wherever he went.

Many years later, the farmer went to church at Christmas with the household, while the woman stayed home, saying she was unwell. On this occasion the farmer had left his key in his everyday clothes, when he put on his best suit. But when he returned home the chest was open, the sealskin gone and the woman too. She had found the key, opened the chest out of curiosity and discovered her sealskin. Then she could not resist the temptation: she bade her children farewell, donned her sealskin and plunged into the sea. Before she went, she is supposed to have said:

> Oh, woe is me,
> I have seven children on land
> and seven in the sea.

The man deeply regretted the loss of his wife, but there was nothing he could do. When he rowed out to fish after that, a seal often swam around his boat and it seemed to have tears in its eyes. After that he always had good catches and many valuable things were washed ashore on his land. And often, when their children walked along the shore, a seal was seen swimming just offshore, keeping pace with them. Not only that, but the seal often tossed up to them many-coloured fishes and pretty shells. But their mother never came ashore again.

41. Gold under Skógafoss

The road eastward across the plains of south Iceland passes through the districts of Ölfus, Flói, Holt, Rangárvellir, Hvolhreppur and Landeyjar. Finally, it crosses the Markarfljót river into Eyjafjallasveit, one of the most picturesque and pleasant regions of Iceland. The landscape there is dominated by the high peaks of Mt. Hekla and the Tindfjallajökull and Eyjafjallajökull glaciers (the latter the tallest peak in the south, at 1,666 m high). Out at sea, the Westman Islands rise up from the ocean depths and from the road by the Seljalandsfoss waterfall they appear to be just offshore.

The coastal lowlands narrow towards the east of the Eyjafjallasveit region and the road passes Hrútafell, Drangshlíðarfjall and Drangshlíðartindur. At Drangshlíð stands a rock, Drangur, from which the place derives its name. According to a folk tale, the semi-legendary Grettir once passed through this area in a bad mood. In his rage, he grabbed a handful of the mountain and flung it westwards onto the lowlands. The rock he threw down is Drangur, while Grettisskarð (Grettir's Pass) is a corresponding gap in the mountain ridge above. Other local place-names include Grettisgluggi (Grettir's Window) and Grettisspor (Grettir's Footprint). Long ago, Drangur was reputed to be the home of elves and other supernatural beings. A sheepshed and cowshed were built up against the rock, and it is said that the farmer did not need to watch over his beasts when they were giving birth, for the elves always took care of them.

Beyond Skóganúpur on the Skógaá river the lowlands broaden once more. Ahead on the right Skógasandur stretches down to the sea; part of these once-barren sands has been successfully planted with grass, resulting in new green fields. On the left below the mountain slope is the hamlet of Skógar and a little farther west is Skógafoss, one of Iceland's most beautiful and impressive waterfalls. There has been a school at Skógar since 1949 and a small community has grown up around it. Skógar also boasts an excellent folk museum, which includes a number of old buildings that have been reconstructed on the site and even a church of the 19th-century type. In the summer holidays, the schoolhouse functions as a hotel.

In recent decades, woods have been planted on the slopes above the school, so that Skógar (Woods) once more lives up to its name. Nothing remains of the woods that originally grew here except the trees on Viðarhólmi (Wood Islet) in the Skógaá river above the waterfall. Farther upstream, the Skógaá river abounds in waterfalls, many of them beautiful, though none to rival Skógafoss. From Skógar a car track leads up on to Skógaheiði, and from there a footpath leads over the Fimmvörðuháls pass and down into the upland valley of Þórsmörk; this is a very popular route with highland walkers.

The first settler at Skógar was named Þrasi Þórólfsson. He was said to be a great warrior, well informed and with supernatural skills. Þrasi had a dispute with Loðmundur the Aged (see p. 148), who had settled at Sólheimar east of the Jökulsá river. Both men had magical powers and their dispute grew ever more rancorous. One after the other, they diverted the Jökulsá river over each other's land, creating the wastelands of Sólheimasandur and Skógasandur. Eventually they saw that neither could win the feud, so they met halfway and agreed that the river should flow the shortest route to the sea. Þrasi made his home just east of Skógafoss: probably he was impressed by the 60 m cascade, since in his old age he took a great chest full of gold and treasure, and threw it under the waterfall. The tale goes as follows:

Þrasi of Skógar was a man of great wealth. When he was old and felt that death was approaching, he decided that he did not want his wealth to be dispersed after his day. So he took a chest full of money and valuable goods, and sank it in the deep pool beneath the Skógafoss waterfall. There the chest has lain for century after century; for a long time, the end of the chest could be seen under the waterfall. Over the ages, many people have tried to lift the chest out but without success. Once it was a near thing, for some brave men managed to get a rope through a ring on the end of the chest. They started hauling the chest up and all went well at first. But then the ring suddenly came off its fastenings and the chest vanished into the depths. All they had left was the ring, which they took back to Skógar.

Skógar used to have a church and the idea arose of fitting the remarkable ring to the church door. But in 1890 the Skógar church was deconsecrated and demolished. The ring from the door found its way to Eyvindarhólar and was fitted to the church door there. In 1960, a new church was built at Eyvindarhólar and the old one demolished. The ring was not used for the new door and so it went to the Skógar Folk Museum, where it is on display, one of the treasures of the museum's collection.

It is probably not worth diving down under Skógafoss in search of Þrasi's treasure-chest, since this is, after all, a folk tale. But there may be a grain of truth in the tale, as witness this old verse that has been passed down from generation to generation:

Richly stacked is Þrasi's chest
under Skógar's waters cold.
Whosoever goes there first
will find wealth untold.

42. Una, the Elf Maid of Rauðafell

Continuing east, the Ring Road approaches the Eyjafjöll mountains. The Eyjafjallajökull glacier is especially impressive, with its peak rising to 1,666 m. About 100 km^2 in area, it is Iceland's sixth-largest glacier. This lofty ice-cap rests on top of a volcanic crater that has been built up through many eruptions, from the middle of the Ice Age until recent times. There is said to have been an eruption under the glacier in 1612 and the volcano also erupted in 1821–23. When the volcano erupts, meltwater from the glacier floods down onto the lowlands north of the mountains.

South and west of the Eyjafjöll mountains is the region known as Eyjafjallasveit, with extensive grassy lowlands and considerable marshy areas. These lowlands were under the sea until the end of the last Ice Age, 10–11,000 years ago, when the glaciers began to melt and the land emerged. The cliffs below the mountains show clear signs of having once been sea cliffs.

There are many farms in the region but it was once far more densely populated, not least due to the fishing. Many people fished from the coast of Eyjafjallasandar into the 20th century.

A long-established farm in the east of the Eyjafjöll region is called Rauðafell (Red Mountain). In the Settlement Age, the place was settled by Hrafn the Foolish. There are many stories of elves in the Eyjafjöll region; the following tale is told of Rauðafell:

Geir was a man who lived at Rauðafell. He was young and energetic, and he had recently lost his wife. One summer at haymaking time, much of the grass had been mown but the women were making slow work of raking the hay. The farmer saw that a tall young woman came and joined the raking women. In the evening she vanished, but returned in the morning and raked all day. This continued all summer; nobody knew where the woman came from or where she went.

On the last day of haymaking, the farmer went to the girl, greeted her and thanked her for her work. She took his thanks well and they talked for a long time. In the end, the farmer engaged her to be his housekeeper. The following morning she arrived at Geir's home, bringing nothing but a big chest, which was placed in the farmer's storeroom. The woman took over the housekeeping tasks and she was hard-working and efficient. She said her name was Una but she would not tell Geir where she was from. She never went to church, although the farmer urged her, for he was a church-going man.

Now Christmas came and everybody went to evening Mass except Una, who chose to stay home and watch over the farm. When the people returned in the morning, Una had finished all the household tasks. Thus she stayed with the farmer for three years and she grew very dear to him. But he was discouraged from marrying her by the fact that she never went to church. There was speculation about Una, who was regarded as the most outstanding woman in the region. Now Christmas approached in the third winter, and again Una stayed home while the rest of the household went to church. When the churchgoers had travelled a little way, the farmhand was suddenly taken ill. He lay down and said he would wait until he felt better. He stayed behind, while the farmer and the other went on. When they were out of sight, the farmhand stood up and went back to the farmhouse – for he had been feigning illness.

Back home he saw Una hurriedly sweeping the floors but

he hid so she did not see him. When she had finished, Una went out to the storeroom and opened her chest. She took out fine clothes and put them on. The farmhand thought he had never seen such a beautiful woman. Then she took a red cloth and went outside. She went down to the fields, followed by the farmhand. Finally, she stopped by a marsh, spread out the red cloth and stepped on to it. The farmhand seized the chance and grabbed one corner of the cloth. They sank down into the earth, as if passing through smoke; she did not notice the farmhand.

Soon they came to green fields, and the farmhand saw a big and splendid farmhouse. Una went there and he followed her. There were many people there who welcomed Una. They sat down to a feast and many dishes and wines were served. The farmhand grabbed a rib of smoked mutton and put it inside his clothes; he had never seen such juicy meat before. After the feast, games were played and all was done with skill and art. As dawn drew near, Una said she had to go, for the farmer would soon be back from church. She bade a solemn farewell and departed on her cloth, along with the farmhand. They went back the way they had come and came up through the earth at the marsh. Una took the cloth home and put it away, along with her best clothes, in the chest in the storeroom.

The farmhand returned to the place where he had feigned illness and was lying there when the farmer returned from church with the others. He said he was fully recovered and went with them. Una welcomed them and soon they sat down to a meal, which included smoked mutton. The farmer took up a great side of mutton and asked: "Has anyone ever seen such a big side of mutton as this?" "Perhaps," said the farmhand and produced the rib he had taken from the feast. When Una saw it, she changed colour and walked away without saying a word. She was never seen again.

No claims will be made here about the truth of this folk tale of the Eyjafjöll region, but below the homefield at Rauðafell there is a place known as Unudý (Una's Marsh).

43. Gilitrutt and the Lazy Wife

The Markarfljót river in the Eyjafjallasveit region was once a hazardous obstacle to travellers. The river was first bridged in 1933, below the farm of Eyvindarholt; this bridge is little used today, as it was superseded some years ago by a modern bridge, farther south, which cuts several kilometres off the route to the east and the Ring Road as a whole. Ahead lie the Eyjafjöll mountains, with their cliffs and waterfalls, capped by the Eyjafjallajökull ice-cap.

To the west of the mountain range is the farm of Stóri-Dalur, once an important manor; in the late 10th century it was the home of Runólfur Úlfsson, the leader of the pagan faction at the Althing (parliament) of AD 1000. The antagonism between pagan and Christian threatened the very existence of the young Icelandic state, and at parliament a decision was made to adopt Christianity. Runólfur himself was baptised, spurred on no doubt by the fact that the belligerent missionary monarch Olaf Tryggvason of Norway had taken his son hostage, along with other young Icelanders, in order to persuade the Icelanders of the benefits of Christianity. On his return home that summer, Runólfur took all his pagan idols and carried them up on to the glacier, where he placed them in a cave in a rock which projects up out of the ice-cap. This has since been called Goðasteinn (Gods' Rock).

In the east of the Eyjafjöll district is Rauðafell, where Hrafn the Foolish settled during the Age of Settlement; he was an ancestor of Sæmundur the Wise, who acquired semi-legendary status in folklore (see p. 176). One of Iceland's favourite folk tales recounts events reputed to have taken place on the farm of Rauðafell: this is the story *of Gilitrutt. Some say she was a troll-wife, while others believe she was an elf woman; above the farmhouse at Rauðafell is a hillock that is supposed to have been Gilitrutt's home, known as Álfhóll (Elf Hill).*

Once upon a time a hardworking farmer lived in the east below the Eyjafjöll mountains. He had recently married a young woman, who was lazy and indolent, and did little work about the farm. The farmer was discontented with this but could do nothing about it. In the autumn, he brought her a great quantity of wool and asked her to weave it into cloth. She was reluctant and as the winter passed she did not touch the wool.

One day a woman of large build came to the farmer's wife and asked her for some favour. The farmer's wife asked her whether she would do something for her in return. The woman asked what that might be and the farmer's wife replied that it was to weave wool into cloth. The woman agreed and the farmer's wife handed her a big sack of wool. The woman slung the sack on to her back and said that she would bring the cloth back on the first day of summer. "What shall I pay you?" asked the farmer's wife. "Nothing much," said the woman. "Tell me what my name is at the third guess and we will be quits." The farmer's wife agreed to these terms and the woman went off with the wool. The winter passed and the farmer often asked where the wool was. His wife replied that it was none of his business and that he would have his woollen cloth on the first day of summer. He was not impressed. Time passed.

As the end of winter approached, the farmer's wife began to think about the woman's name; she could see no way of finding it out and grew melancholy over this. The farmer noticed that she was unhappy, came to her and asked what was wrong. Then she told him the whole story. The farmer was frightened and said that the woman was probably a troll-wife, who would take her away.

Some time later, the farmer was walking below the mountain slope, when he came to a stony hillock. He was deep in thought and feeling unhappy, when he heard a knocking sound inside the hillock and went closer. Finally, he found a gap in the rock and saw a large woman sitting inside, energetically weaving at a loom she held between her legs as she chanted:

Hi, ho, hi, ho,
the farmer's wife doesn't know my name.
Gilitrutt's my name, Gilitrutt's my name.
Hi, ho, hi, ho.

The farmer was cheered by this; he was sure this must be the woman who had visited his wife last autumn. He went home in a good mood and made a note of the name Gilitrutt. But he did not tell his wife what he had seen and heard. Time passed and finally the last day of winter came around. By now the farmer's wife was so distraught that she could not get out of bed. Her husband came to her and asked if she knew the name of her helper. She said she did not and that this would be the end of her. Then the farmer comforted her, told her all that had happened, and gave her the piece of paper with the name on it. She took the paper, trembling with terror, for she feared the name might be wrong. She asked her husband to stay with her when the woman arrived but the farmer refused; he said that she alone had made the pact about the wool, so she alone must pay the fee.

On the morning of the first day of summer, the woman lay alone in her bed; there was no one else in the house. Then she heard a great din and heavy footsteps. The large woman entered, looking far from friendly. She flung down a great roll of woollen cloth and asked: "So what's my name? What's my name?" The farmer's wife was terrified almost to death, but stammered the name "Ása." "Guess again, guess again, farmer's wife," said the woman. "Signý." "One more guess, one more guess, farmer's wife," said the woman. Then the farmer's wife plucked up courage and asked: "I don't suppose your name is Gilitrutt?" The woman was so startled that she fell down flat on the floor with a great crash. Then she jumped to her feet, rushed out and was never seen again. The farmer's wife was delighted at her escape from the creature and she changed her ways completely. She became a hardworking and conscientious farmwife, and she always wove her own wool after that.

44. The Sea Ghost at Hvammsnúpur

At Seljalandsmúli in the Eyjafjöll district there is a view towards the east, to the cliffs at the edge of the mountain range. Some distance east of Seljaland is a farm called Sauðhúsvöllur and a little farther east a small cluster of hillocks, Hafurshóll. This was a popular stopping-place for travellers in the past, but today the road lies to the south of the hillocks and now few passers-by halt there. Hafurshóll was believed to be inhabited by elves and there were several spots where the grass was never mown; on winter evenings, lights were often seen there, in the windows of elf homes.

Just east of Hafurshóll and southwest of the steep cliffs of Hvammsnúpur is the farm of Hvammur, where verdant slopes stretch up from the farmhouse to the towering cliffs above. Below Hvammsnúpur lie several rocky hillocks known as Pöst and Dysjarhóll, where ankaramite, a rare form of basalt, is found. In former times, the main route through the region passed through the homefield at Hvammur and along the steep slope beneath Hvammsnúpur, while the Markarfljót river flowed directly below. Long ago, a ghost known as Flóðalabbi (the Sea Ghost) used to haunt the road, playing pranks on those who followed the narrow and dangerous path. He would snatch the baggage off their packhorses and fling it into the fast-flowing river below. An old tale tells of the ghost:

Once upon a time there lived a farmer at Hvammur below the Eyjafjöll mountains. His name is not known but he was said to be so strong and brave that he was a match for two men. Once he went down to the shore and found a dead man washed up by the sea. The dead man wore a gown and boots and was finely dressed, but the farmer paid him no respect and robbed the corpse of everything of value. Then he took the body home and had it buried at Holt, his parish church. This was in winter and everything was covered in snow and ice. It happened one evening, after the dead man had been buried, that the farmer went out late, at about the time the women went to the cowshed to milk the cows. He did not return that night and in the morning a search was made. There were many tracks in the snow south of the farmhouse. The Markarfljót river, which flowed east of Hvammsleira in those days, was thickly frozen over. The tracks led southwards, across the river, and farther south there were bloodstains on the snow. The tracks led south towards the sea, where the farmer was found dead. His back was broken and he had several wounds. He was then buried and did no one any harm. But after that the dead man whose corpse had been washed ashore was always walking and was deemed an evil guest. He came to be known as Flóðalabbi (Sea Ghost).

As the Markarfljót flowed in those days east of Hvammsleira into the Rimhúsaáll river, all travellers went east of Hvammsnúpur along a narrow footpath. Flóðalabbi would loiter near the footpath and play pranks on those who passed by, hauling the baggage off the packhorses and so on. Nobody dared travel there except in broad daylight and preferably in a group. Once the pastor of Holt was passing by; he had excellent horses. When he made to ride eastward from Hvammsnúpur, however, his mount stood stock still at the most hazardous place on the path and would not move. The pastor eventually grew tired of this and struck the horse between the ears with his whip. The horse jumped more than the height of a man into the air and did not stop until he reached home at Holt. The pastor believed that Flóðalabbi had stood in the way of the horse (although he could not see him himself) and that the horse had leapt over the ghost.

In the summer, the local farmers went to the market town with their wares, as usual, including the Rev. Magnús of Hörgsland. He called at Holt on his way along the mountain range, while the rest of the travellers went on ahead. When the pastor's companions reached Hvammsnúpur, there was Flóðalabbi and he hauled the baggage off all the horses. When they replaced it, he dragged it off again. Among the goods that fell into the river were casks of butter that the pastor was taking to market. This continued until the Rev. Magnús arrived. He asked his companions to reload the horses and said that Flóðalabbi would hardly dare drag them off while he was there. The pastor asked them to go on to their next stopping-place. They were to wait for him until noon the following day; if he had not arrived by then, there would be little point in waiting any longer.

While the pastor turned his attention to Flóðalabbi, the pack train went to Djúpidalur by the eastern Rangá river, struggling here and there in the marsh which is nearby, to the east. Whatever happened, the pastor did not reach the campsite of his companions until next morning; he was very dazed. He later said that he had had a hard time with the ghost. The main problem was that the ghost was a good versifier. The Rev. Magnús said that he had spoken verses in the ten languages he knew and Flóðalabbi had answered in as many tongues – but the pastor did not know the language Flóðalabbi knew best. Yet in the end the Rev. Magnús was victorious. When Flóðalabbi had sunk so far into the marsh that only his head was visible, he had asked the pastor to step on his head before they parted. The pastor did this, but he feared Flóðalabbi's trickery and so he cut his shoelace first. Flóðalabbi then sank into the marsh with the shoe but as he went down he grabbed at the nearby rocks, where the marks left by his fingers can still be seen. Finally, the pastor laid Flóðalabbi to rest so that he would not walk again, and indeed he has never been seen since.

45. Snorri the Fugitive

The route continues through south Iceland to Þórsmörk, an upland valley that is a favourite with tourists; Þórsmörk boasts mountains and valleys, wildflowers and birch woods, glacial rivers and crystal-clear streams, grassland and barren sands. Majestic glaciers rise up on three sides of this mountain fastness. But natural beauty is not the only attraction for visitors to Þórsmörk: for those on the folklore trail there is also a cave of special interest, named Snorraríki, in Húsadalur.

To reach the cave, turn off the Ring Road just east of the Markarfljót river and follow a rough mountain road into the north of the Eyjafjöll mountain range. The route is surrounded by magnificent landscape: to the left the Tindafjöll mountains and to the right the Eyjafjallajökull ice-cap, while ahead lies the Mýrdalsjökull glacier in the uplands east of Þórsmörk.

There is a glacial lagoon at the foot of the Gígjökull glacial tongue, which plunges down the steep mountainside like a waterfall. Ice floes calve from the glacier from time to time, to float on the opaque waters of the lagoon. The road continues across the Steinholtsá river and the barren lowlands named Fagriskógur after the long-vanished woods that once grew there. It is worth stopping at the Stakkholtsgjá gorge, one of the most spectacular natural formations in this region. From there, the route crosses the Hvanná river to Goðaland, south of the Krossá river. The landscape here is picturesque, especially at Básar, which has a lodge and campsite for visitors.

It is necessary to turn off the road in order to ford the Krossá river *into Þórsmörk proper; this dangerous and fast-flowing river should only be crossed with the greatest care.*

This route leads to Langidalur in Þórsmörk, which has an excellent lodge for visitors. To the left is the Valahnjúkur peak (458 m), which is climbed by many visitors to Þórsmörk, as it commands splendid views. It is also possible to take a walk over to Húsadalur (Houses' Valley), which was once inhabited. In the Saga Age, this was the home of Björn Kaðalsson the White, who plays a part in Njál's Saga. *From the head of Langidalur, the path leads up on to a ridge, then down into Húsadalur. High on the slope is a basalt cliff and high up in this cliff is a cave known as Snorraríki (Snorri's Dominion):*

There was once a man named Snorri, who was probably both young and strong, for he proved most resourceful. He had stolen something or committed some other offence, so that he found himself on the wrong side of the law. At that time the criminal code was both harsh and merciless, so Snorri decided to avoid the royal officials and ran away. A posse was raised to follow him and capture him, but the men soon found that Snorri was quick on his feet and evaded them all. He fled into the mountains, to Þórsmörk. There, Snorri was overtaken by the searchers and they finally succeeded in cornering him, so it appeared that he had no way out. But when they tried to capture this fleet-footed man, he climbed up into a cave at the top of Húsadalur. The search party soon found out where he was and decided to surround the cave and starve Snorri into submission. They could not reach him there, for the cave is so high up in the rock that one man can easily defend himself, though besieged by many. And so the search party decided to wait at the foot of the cliff until Snorri grew so hungry that he would give himself up.

But things did not go as they had foreseen. They waited there, day after day and night after night, and Snorri the fugitive showed no signs of surrendering. This had gone on for a long time and they thought that Snorri would soon succumb to starvation, when the fugitive suddenly appeared at the mouth of the cave. But he was not there to give himself up; instead, he threw a good, fat leg of lamb down to the exhausted men below and said he hoped they enjoyed it. The men were taken aback and said that there was no point in trying to starve Snorri into submission; he had so much food that he was sharing it with them! After some consultation, they decided to abandon the siege and return home.

What they did not know was that the leg of lamb Snorri had flung down to them was the only food left in the cave. He did this as a last resort and it had the desired result. When the posse had gone, Snorri climbed down from the cave and made his escape. No more is known of Snorri but such a resourceful man must surely have been able to take care of himself. After this the cave was known as Snorraríki (Snorri's Dominion), in honour of the resourceful and fleet-footed fugitive.

Today, steps have been cut into the rock, so almost anyone can climb up to Snorri's Dominion – provided he or she is wearing good walking shoes and has a head for heights. Many visitors to Þórsmörk have carved their name, initials or the date in the rock below the cave, and perhaps the initials of Snorri himself are somewhere among them. Who knows?

46. The Pastor of Súlnasker

Off the south coast of Iceland rise the Vestmannaeyjar (Westman Islands), an archipelago of 15 islands, plus another 30 rocks and skerries. Only the largest of the islands, Heimaey, is inhabited – and has been since the early days of Iceland's history. In the past, there was considerable animal husbandry on the islands, while the islanders also lived off the excellent nearby fishing grounds, and hunted birds and gathered eggs on the many bird cliffs. In more recent times, the fisheries have become the pillar of the islands' economy and the fishing town of Vestmannaeyjar on Heimaey island has grown to number nearly 5,000 people.

The Westman Islands have a long and colourful history. In the 15th and 16th centuries, Englishmen and other foreigners fished and traded there, not always in the spirit of peaceful coexistence. The islands also fell prey to pirates, for instance in the so-called "Turkish Raid" of 1627, when Algerian pirates raided the islands and took over 200 islanders captive, to sell them in the slave markets of North Africa. In 1973, a volcanic eruption on Heimaey island forced all the inhabitants to flee to the mainland and buried one third of the town under lava. But the islanders returned after the eruption to rebuild their town.

The islands are also rich in folklore. One tale tells of the pastor of Súlnasker – a tiny skerry only 0.03 km^2 in area, near the south of the archipelago.

Súlnasker (Gannet Skerry) is so called for its large gannet colony and is sometimes also termed the Good Skerry. It deserves this name, for the Westman Islanders catch four to five thousand fulmars and four to five hundred gannets there every year. The skerry is also the islanders' most abundant source of seabird eggs. It stands up out of the sea on four rock pillars, so high that one may row under it, if the sea is calm. The skerry is visited once a year for bird catching. The bird catchers must pick a fine day, for there is heavy surf at the skerry and the route up on to it is also very hazardous. The day when the skerry is visited is a kind of festival for the islanders. They are always cheerful on that day, provided that no one is hurt and the catches are good.

The skerry slopes considerably to the southwest, and a story tells why this is so: originally, no one even considered climbing up on to the skerry, for it seemed quite inaccessible, except to a bird on the wing. In the end, however, two brave men made the attempt successfully, though it was a hazardous journey. The man who first made it on to the skerry said: "Here I am, by God's grace," while the other said: "Here I am, whether God wills or no." At that, the skerry tipped sideways and flung the godless man into the depths, where he was lost forever. But a large man appeared and caught hold of the other man, and kept him from falling too. From that day, the skerry has sloped; the large man was the pastor of the skerry. He helped the islander down off the skerry and also assisted him in making a path up on to it. This path was used for a long time but today it has been abandoned in favour of a better one.

In former times, the skerry pastor was reputed to wave to the islanders when they came to land on the skerry and to signal to them to turn away if bad weather was on the way. If they ignored his signals, something invariably went wrong: the ship was damaged, a man injured or the like. Sometimes, in spite of bad weather at the skerry, he signalled them to land and then the wind always died down and the sea grew calm. For this, the islanders were most grateful to the skerry pastor; even today, when someone arrives on the skerry for the first time, he leaves some coins in a stone container there. These are intended as a gift to the pastor and on the next visit they are always gone.

In addition to this, the skerry priest is said to be an excellent pastor and a good preacher of true doctrine. Otherwise he could not be such a good friend of the pastor of Ofanleiti, on Heimaey island. The skerry pastor visits the pastor of Ofanleiti once a year, rowing his stone boat to Ofanleiti on New Year's Eve. The pastor welcomes him warmly, with coffee, liquor, smoked mutton and other delicacies. When the skerry priest departs again from Ofanleiti, the local pastor sees him to his boat. They go down at midnight to the bay where the skerry pastor beaches his boat and the two launch it together.

In recent years, the skerry priest is said to be seen less often than before. Some say that he must have grown old, so that he cannot travel any more. But no one has heard of another pastor taking over the benefice or of the old pastor appointing a chaplain.

47. Herjólfur and Vilborg of the Westman Islands

The Westman Islands lie off the south coast of Iceland; there are 15 islands including Surtsey, which was formed in a volcanic eruption on the sea floor in 1963, as well as about 30 rocks and skerries. The only inhabited island is Heimaey, the largest. North of Heimaey are Bjarnarey and Elliðaey; to the south Suðurey, Álsey, Hellisey, Súlnasker, Brandur, Geldungur and Geirfuglasker; and to the west of Heimaey the islets of Hani, Hæna, Hrauney and Grasleysa. In geological terms the islands are young, all formed by volcanic activity between the end of the last Ice Age, 10,000 years ago, and 1963, when Surtsey was formed. Most of the islands are surrounded by steep sea cliffs and many have interesting caves, such as Klettshellir in Ystiklettur, Kafhellir on Hæna, Fjósin on Stórhöfði, etc. The islands are famed for their bird cliffs and the millions of birds that nest in them. In times past, the seabirds and their eggs were a vital resource for the islanders.

On Heimaey island, 13.4 km^2 in area, is the town of Vestmannaeyjar, with a population of just under 5,000. Heimaey boasts a varied landscape. Heimaklettur, the highest point on the islands, rises to 283 m above sea level. Other peaks on the island are Ystiklettur, Miðklettur, Klifið, Háin, Dalfjall, Helgafell, Stórhöfði and Eldfell, which was formed in the Heimaey eruption of 1973.

The history of the Westman Islands begins, according to the Book of Settlements, at the very start of the settlement of Iceland, when

Ingólfur Arnarson and his sworn brother, Hjörleifur, were searching for a place to settle in Iceland. Some Irish slaves belonging to Hjörleifur slew their master and several other free men, then fled to the offshore islands. Ingólfur soon chased after them and took his revenge, naming the islands Vestmannaeyjar (Westman Islands) after the Irish or "West Men". Before long, the islands were settled like the rest of Iceland. In the 12th century, they came into the possession of the episcopate of Skálholt; the bishop, Magnús Einarsson, planned to establish a monastery on the islands but this plan came to nothing when he died in a fire in 1148. In the early 15th century, the islands passed to the King of Denmark and remained a royal possession until 1874.

Royal authority was a heavy burden on the islanders, due to the obligation to man royal fishing boats, the restrictions of the Danish trade monopoly, and so forth. The Westman Islands were an important fishing port over the centuries, as there were rich fishing grounds nearby. The English began to fish in Icelandic waters in the 15th century and soon the Germans followed suit; conflict often arose between the two factions, not least in the Westman Islands.

The worst disaster in the history of the islands was the so-called "Turkish Raid" of 1627, when Algerian pirates raided the islands, killing and maiming, and took more than 200 islanders captive. They were subsequently sold into slavery in Algiers. A handful of these captives were later ransomed and released, among them Guðríður Símonardóttir, known as "Gudda of the Turks", who eventually married Hallgrímur Pétursson, one of Iceland's best-loved poets. After the "Turkish Raid", old coastal fortifications were rebuilt; this structure is known as Skansinn.

Herjólfsdalur is a picturesque valley west of the town beneath Mt. Dalfjall. In 1874, when the Icelanders celebrated the millennium of the settlement of Iceland and the granting of a constitution by the King of Denmark, the Westman Islanders held their celebrations in Herjólfsdalur. These celebrations were repeated in 1900 and since then a summer festival has been held on the islands on the first weekend in August each year, during which Herjólfsdalur is lit up and decorated. But this valley is not only known for the annual summer festival – it has a much longer history. The valley bears the name of the first settler on the Westman Islands, a certain Herjólfur, who made his home *in Herjólfsdalur (Herjólfur's Valley). In the valley is a small pond, formed from a spring named Lindin (The Spring), which was reputed to be the best source of water on the islands:*

Once upon a time there lived a man named Herjólfur in the valley on the Westman Islands that has been known since then as Herjólfsdalur. He was the only one of the islanders who had a good water source near his farmhouse, so many people came to him to ask for water, for which he demanded payment. Herjólfur had a daughter named Vilborg. She was unlike her father in character. He had a reputation for driving a hard bargain when he insisted on payment for water but Vilborg often secretly gave people water at night, without her father's knowledge.

One day Vilborg was outside the farmhouse repairing shoes, when a raven came to her, took one of the shoes and flew away with it. She did not want to lose the shoe, so she followed the raven. When she had gone a little way from the farmhouse, a landslide fell from the mountain on to Herjólfur's house and her father was killed. Thus Vilborg owed her life to the raven, to which she had often been kind.

After the landslide, Vilborg, daughter of Herjólfur, did not wish to live at the old farmhouse any more and she is said to have built a new farmhouse, called Vilborgarstaðir. She declared that a pond south of the farmhouse should be named Vilpa and that the water from Vilpa should harm no one, even though it did not always appear wholesome. Vilborg is said to have been buried in the western part of the homefield at Vilborgarstaðir, at a place that is still called Borguleiði (Vilborg's Grave).

In Herjólfsdalur, above the rocks that fell on the farmhouse, there is still a clear spring which never runs dry, even when there is a lack of water elsewhere on the island. This is supposed to be the same spring from which Herjólfur sold the water, while his kind-hearted daughter gave the water away when she could.

48. Sæmundur the Wise and the Devil

On its way across south Iceland, the Ring Road passes through Rangárvellir, the extensive lowlands between the two Rangá rivers. The mountain landscape is spectacular, especially Mt. Hekla, the Tindafjöll mountain range and the Eyjafjallajökull ice-cap. Further east, between the villages of Hella and Hvolsvöllur, the Ring Road passes the ancient manor of Oddi in the lowlands to the right. Oddi has had a church and resident pastor for many centuries and in the days of the Old Commonwealth (930–1262) it was one of Iceland's major centres of culture and power.

Sæmundur Sigfússon (1056–1133) served the parish of Oddi and laid the foundation for the power of the Oddi clan in centuries to come. His sons (clerical celibacy was not required in those days) included Eyjólfur, a priest and school principal, and Loftur, who married Þóra, the daughter of King Magnus the Bare-Legged of Norway. Their son was Jón Loftsson of Oddi, who ruled over Iceland in his time like an uncrowned monarch.

A school was early founded at Oddi, where boys were trained for the priesthood; one of its most famous alumni was Þorlákur Þórhallsson (d. 1193), who went on to become bishop of Skálholt and was canonised (though only in Iceland) after his death. Another famous pupil of the Oddi School was Snorri Sturluson (d. 1241), who was sent at a young age to be brought up by Jón Loftsson, and went on to be a great scholar as well as a powerful worldly magnate. The Oddi clan went into decline in the 13th century and its power died out after Iceland came under Norwegian rule in 1262.

Many remarkable pastors have served at Oddi over the centuries, and not a few of them have gone on to wear the bishop's cope. The best known of the latter-day pastors at Oddi was the poet Matthías Jochumsson, who served the parish 1881–1887. He wrote, among other things, the words to Iceland's national anthem.

But by far the best known of the clerics who have served at Oddi is Sæmundur Sigfússon, known as "the Wise", of whom many folk tales are told. He travelled abroad at a young age to study and is reputed to have been the first Nordic student at the Sorbonne in Paris – known in Icelandic as the "Black School" because it was reputed to teach "black" arts. He later played an important role in the government of Iceland. He is also reputed to have been a pioneer of Icelandic literature, writing a history of the Norse kings in Latin. None of his writings have survived, but writers of past centuries often make reference to Sæmundur's works, so they must certainly have existed.

Among the tales of Sæmundur the Wise are the following:

At the Black School, the Devil himself was headmaster and here men learned magic and other ancient mysteries. When the students graduated from this school, the custom was that the Devil kept the one who was last to leave. Sæmundur volunteered to be last to leave in his group of graduates and his fellow students were most relieved. He donned a big coat, with the sleeves loose and all the buttons undone. At the door the Devil grabbed at him and said: "You are mine." But the coat came loose and the Devil was left holding it while Sæmundur made his escape.

After his time at the Black School, Sæmundur had grown so skilled that he could use the Devil to perform various errands for him and he tricked him so that the Devil got little or nothing for his trouble. Sæmundur wanted to be appointed to the benefice of Oddi, which was available at that time, but there were many candidates for the office, so Sæmundur wanted to get there as quickly as possible, for he was still abroad. He called the Devil to him and said: "Swim with me to Iceland, and if you can get me ashore there without wetting my gown in the sea, I will be at your mercy." The Devil took him at his word, assumed the shape of a seal and swam with Sæmundur on his back. Sæmundur was reading the Psalter all the way. Before long they were close to Iceland. Then Sæmundur struck the seal on the head with the Psalter, so the seal sank. Sæmundur went under the water, then swam for land and came ashore dripping wet. And thus the Devil lost the bargain, while Sæmundur was appointed to Oddi.

Once Father Sæmundur asked the Devil how small he could make himself. The Devil said he could make himself as small as a midge. Then Sæmundur took a drill and drilled a hole in a pillar and told the Devil to go into the hole. The Devil was quick to do as he asked; then Sæmundur put a stopper in the hole and however much the Devil howled and shrieked and begged for mercy, Sæmundur would not remove the stopper until the Devil promised to serve him and always do as he wished. This was why Sæmundur could always make the Devil do as he pleased.

Once Sæmundur lacked a cowhand and he had the Devil do the work. As the winter passed, the Devil did his work excellently but when Sæmundur was celebrating Mass on Easter Sunday, the Devil moved the whole dunghill and put it in front of the church door, so the priest could not get out after Mass. Sæmundur called the Devil to him and forced him to take all the dung away and return it to its rightful place. He was so harsh that he finally made him lick up the last traces with his tongue. The Devil licked so hard that he made a hollow in the paving stone in front of the church door. This paving stone is said to be still in existence at Oddi today, though only one-fourth of the original stone – and the hollow made by the Devil's tongue – remains clearly visible.

The Devil was often enraged with Sæmundur the Wise, for he resented the way that Sæmundur always got the better of him. He did all he could to be revenged upon him. Once he changed himself into a fly and hid under the skin on top of the milk in the priest's eating-bowl; he planned to get inside the priest and kill him. But the priest saw the fly, wound it up in the skin and then tied it up in a caul and placed the package on the altar in the church. The fly had to stay there during the priest's next service. At the end of Mass, the pastor opened the package and released the Devil. It is said that the Devil never felt more miserable than when he had to lie on the altar while Father Sæmundur officiated at Mass.

49. Gissur of Botnar and the Troll-wife

No one who travels through the south of Iceland can help noticing Mt. Hekla, Iceland's most beautiful and best-known volcano. The mountain rises up from the lowlands north of Rangárvellir and dominates the landscape all around. Hekla is believed to have been formed about 7,000 years ago, when the first fissure eruption occurred on the site, and its splendid mass has been built up gradually during at least 100 eruptions. In the 1,100 years since Iceland was settled, Hekla erupted an average of twice each century, until the 20th century, when it erupted six times: a very large eruption in 1947, another in 1970, and small eruptions in 1980, 1981, 1991 and 2000. In the past, eruptions of Mt. Hekla were believed to presage important events, such as wars or the deaths of kings and emperors. Although such beliefs are rare today, it is interesting to note that the 1991 eruption started on 17 January, the same day as the Gulf War began and King Olaf V of Norway died.

The innermost farm on Rangárvellir is Næfurholt, which lies close to the volcano. Nearby is a picturesque, steep-sloped hill named Bjólfell. North of Næfurholt, far above the inhabited areas, is a great gorge named Tröllkonugil (Troll-wife's Gorge). West of the Þjórsá river, farther inland than Bjólfell, is a table mountain named Búrfell.

To reach the troll-wife's gorge, travellers should set out eastwards through the southern lowlands, crossing the Ölfusá river at Selfoss and the Þjórsá river at Þjótandi. The route turns left at Landvegamót, heading northwards through the Holt and Land districts. This road continues northwards across the uplands via Sprengisandur, but those intent *on reaching the gorge should continue through Landsveit, drawing ever closer to Mt. Hekla, Bjólfell and Búrfell. There, the route passes the innermost farms of Landsveit – Skarð, Stóri-Klofi, Leirubakki and Galtalækur – and soon reaches the sand and pumice desert laid waste by eruptions of Mt. Hekla. This is the territory of the troll-wife of Búrfell:*

Once upon a time there were two troll-wives: one lived in Mt. Búrfell and the other in Mt. Bjólfell. They were sisters and close friends. The troll-wife of Búrfell often visited her sister, travelling east across the Þjórsá and Rangá rivers to Bjólfell, and her sister probably visited her too. Búrfell is a very rocky mountain with steep cliffs. To the east, below the middle of the hill, there are two rocks, not very high, one on either side of the Þjórsá river. Two more rocks, about the same height, stand up out of the river between them, so the river cascades down in three branches. The troll-wife of Búrfell is said to have placed these stepping-stones in the river so that she could cross it in three jumps without wetting her feet. The rocks are called Tröllkonuhlaup (Troll-wife's Leap).

Kjallakatungur is the name of an area of sand dunes and vegetation between the Þjórsá and Rangá rivers. In former times, those who travelled north to the upland pastures passed through this area.

In Landsveit there is a farm named Botnar or Lækjarbotnar. The farmer living there when this story took place was named Gissur. One day he went in to the uplands to go fishing, taking a packhorse along. When he felt he had caught as many fish as the horse could carry, he set off homewards. Nothing is known of his journey until he reached Kjallakatungur opposite Tröllkonuhlaup, where he heard a voice thundering out of Búrfell:

"Sister, lend me a cooking pot."

"What do you want it for?" was asked from Bjólfell.

"To cook a man in it," resounded from Búrfell.

“What’s his name?” was asked from Bjólfell.

“Gissur of Botnar, Gissur of Lækjarbotnar,” was heard from Búrfell.

At that moment Farmer Gissur looked up at Búrfell and saw a troll-wife come clattering down the slope, heading straight for Tröllkonuhlaup. He was convinced that she meant to put her words into action and that he must try to escape. He released the packhorse and whipped the one he was riding, a fine, light-footed mount. He rode as fast as he could, without looking back, but he could hear the troll-wife panting after him and concluded that she was catching up.

Gissur rode down through Land, with the troll-wife hard on his heels. Then he was fortunate that the people of Klofi saw him and the troll-wife, and rang all the church bells at Klofi just as Gissur reached the homefield. The troll-wife, having failed to catch Gissur, flung her axe after him; as he reached the farmhouse, his horse dropped down dead with the axe blade buried in its loins. Gissur gave sincere thanks to God for his escape from peril.

As for the troll-wife, she was so taken aback by the ringing of the bells that she went mad and ran away as fast as she could. She was seen from various farms in Land. She ran much farther than her home, heading eastwards towards Tröllkonugil; she was found there, dead of exertion, a few days later and the gully has been known since then as Tröllkonugil (Troll-wife’s Gorge). Her sister of Bjólfell is not known to have threatened her neighbours and little is told of her after the demise of her sister. Some say that she moved to Tröllkonugil, not wishing to live so close to humans any more.

50. The Green Valley in the Glacier

In the uplands of south Iceland there is an area of geothermal activity known as Landmannalaugar (laugar = hot springs). This picturesque and beautiful spot attracts growing numbers of visitors, and a campsite, huts and other facilities are available there. Above the hot-spring area is Laugahraun, a dark expanse of obsidian lava, while around Landmannalaugar rise rhyolite mountains in a varied palette of pale colours; the best known of these are Barmur, Bláhnjúkur and Brennisteinsalda. The valley of Landmannalaugar abounds in springs, both hot and cold; these feed a deep and slow-flowing stream, which is comfortably warm for bathing and swimming. To the southeast of Landmannalaugar lies a gorge named Jökulgil, running south to the Torfajökull glacier. This was once believed to be a refuge for outlaws; when farmers did not succeed in rounding up all their sheep from the summer pastures, the outlaws were generally blamed. In 1852 the gorge was finally explored and after this it was regularly searched during the autumn round-up. No outlaws were found but the farmers did tend to find more sheep by searching the gorge.

But according to old tales, the gorge was indeed inhabited for a time, when District Commissioner Torfi Jónsson of Klofi moved his household there during the Black Death that scourged Iceland in 1494–95. The plague is said to have been brought to Iceland by English merchants who called at Hafnarfjörður, near Reykjavík, and people believed that it was spread in the form of a blue miasma. It was said that the disease struck so rapidly that women were found dead at their milking-pails or over the casks in their larders. On many farms *only two or three people were spared. There might be three or four funerals a day, and if six or seven people attended a funeral, only two or three returned alive; the rest died on the way, or were buried in the graves they had dug for others. Torfi sought some way of safeguarding himself and his household from this terrible pestilence:*

When District Commissioner Torfi learned that the pestilence had arrived east of the Hellisheiði heath, he gathered up his belongings and went away from Klofi with all that he could transport. He moved with his household to the upland pastures of the men of the Land district. To the south of the pastures is a glacier that stands alone, east of Mt. Hekla. Torfi went there with his household and goods. He travelled eastwards along the north of the glacier until he reached a brook. Along the brook was fertile and beautiful land, where the grass was so tall that it bent under its own weight. Torfi travelled up the gorge, now called Jökulgil (Glacier Gorge), through which the brook flows. Soon the grass grew sparse and the land barren. Torfi's retainers said among themselves that they would prefer to stay on the grassland down by the brook, which they thought was quite a good place to live, and that Torfi would hardly find a better place by going on up this black gorge almost completely enclosed by cliffs. When Torfi heard the mutterings of his retainers, he told them to leave the decision to him, since he had managed to make good provision for them hitherto.

After this they went on up the gorge. When they had walked for a while, they saw a bright light from the south. The gorge then widened out once more and they found themselves in a fair, broad valley that appeared to lie along the length of the glacier from east to west. There was not a single gap in the cliffs around it, except where they had come in at the north, where the brook flowed out of the valley. Around the valley there was nothing to be seen but glacier and blue sky, while below the cliff edges, wooded slopes led right down to the lowlands, with their smooth, beautiful, grassy plains. "Let us stay here awhile," said Torfi. "The blue miasma must indeed be noxious, if it can harm us in this valley." After this, Torfi set his men to work to build a house – and he had plenty of farmhands at his disposal.

During the summer, Torfi had his workers cultivate the valley and the farm flourished due to the remarkable qualities of the land. Though Torfi warned his men against contact with the people of the district below, every two weeks he sent two men he trusted down to the edge of the mountain range, where they could see the farms below, so that they could report on the blue miasma that brought the plague. But for a long time they always returned with the discouraging news that the miasma was still there, reaching halfway up the mountain slopes, and that nobody was to be seen. But at last the time came when the emissaries brought the news that the miasma was gone. Torfi remained in the valley for a while longer, however, until he felt sure that the plague was gone for good. Then he packed up his possessions and returned to his home at Klofi. Neither he nor any of his household suffered any harm from the pestilence.

The story does not tell how long Torfi stayed up in the glacier, which has been known as Torfajökull (Torfi's Glacier) ever since. When Torfi set off to return home, some of his retainers did not want to leave the valley, and he allowed them to stay on, giving them the house he had had built. Ever since then, until recent times, it was said that there were outlaws on the Torfajökull glacier, and travellers on the Fjallabak route to Skaftafellssýsla were reputed to smell woodsmoke there. When farmers did not manage to find all their sheep during the autumn round-up, these outlaws were often blamed. But many years ago, when the men of the Land district went and explored the Jökulgil gorge, it was proved that the loss of sheep could not be attributed to outlaws on the glacier. The men travelled far enough to see that the once-green valley was now full of ice and snow, and quite uninhabitable; it was no longer grassy and wooded as in the days of Torfi at Klofi.

51. Jóra of Jórukleif

The journey eastwards from Reykjavík across the Hellisheiði heath on the Ring Road is a quick one; before long, the road descends the steep Kambar to Hveragerði and then continues eastwards, passing through the gateway between Kögunarhóll and Silfurberg, the southernmost point of Mt. Ingólfsfjall. The view from here includes the southern lowlands, the peaks of Mt. Hekla and Tindafjöll, and the Eyjafjallajökull ice-cap, while offshore the Westman Islands rise up from the depths. The road soon reaches Selfoss, a growing town on the banks of the Ölfusá river, which developed during the 20th century after the river was bridged. The Ölfusá bridge, opened on 8 September 1891, was the first of Iceland's modern bridges and heralded the nation's entrance into the modern age.

The construction of the bridge was largely due to the efforts of the entrepreneur and parliamentarian Tryggvi Gunnarsson. Tryggvaskáli (Tryggvi's Cabin), constructed to provide facilities for the bridge-builders, was the first building on the site where Selfoss stands today. Once the bridge was opened, refreshments for travellers were provided at Tryggvaskáli and before long other commercial ventures were established in the new community. In 1930 the population of Selfoss numbered 68; this number rose by the turn of the century to more than 4,000.

Originally a part of the surrounding rural districts, Selfoss became a separate administrative unit in 1947 and in 1978 it received its town charter. The bridge constructed in 1891 was intended for pedestrians and horses; in the early 20th century motor traffic began to use *the bridge, which sustained the additional strain for many years before collapsing in 1944 under the weight of two lorries. Remarkably, no lives were lost when the old bridge gave way. A new bridge was completed in December 1945.*

A short distance above the Ölfusá bridge, two rocks project up out of the river; there were originally three but one was swept away in a flood in 1959. The rocks, known as Jóruhlaup (Jóra's Leap), derive their name from a certain Jórunn (diminutive Jóra) who was a farmer's daughter on a nearby farm long ago:

Once upon a time there was a girl named Jórunn who lived on a farm in the Sandvík district of Flói. She was young and promising, but of difficult character. Once a horse fight was held in the district; her father owned one of the horses that competed. Jórunn attended the horse fight and saw that her father's horse was beaten. She grew so mad with rage that she rushed over to the other horse and tore off one of its legs. She ran off with the leg at full speed to the Ölfusá river, to a waterfall – either the Laxfoss or Selfoss falls. There she tore great chunks from the rocks and flung them almost to the middle of the river. She crossed the river by these stepping-stones and said:

> Fitting steps for a maid to make,
> time for her a groom to take.

The place has been known since then as Jóruhlaup (Jóra's Leap). After this feat she continued up through the Ölfus district east of Mt. Ingólfsfjall and into Grafningur, until she reached a gully that lies to the west of Grafningur. She ran up the gully until she reached Mt. Hengill, where she made her home in Jóruhellir (Jóra's Cave) and became the worst of trolls, devouring both men and beasts. It was her custom to walk up to a peak in the Hengill mountain range, where she would sit for hours at a time. The place has since been called Jórusöðull (Jóra's Saddle). From there she watched for people passing and then ambushed the travellers in a gully known ever since as Jórukleif (Jóra's Ridge). She captured men and killed them for food, once she had finished the horse's haunch. She soon grew so evil and wild that the farms around her were laid waste and the paths through the region were abandoned. This was a very harmful thing and forces were gathered to slay Jóra, but without success.

When this difficult situation had arisen and there appeared to be no way of defeating Jóra or driving her away, a young man came up with a solution. He was travelling between countries and spent a year in Norway. One day he went to the king and told him of this evil being which had made its home in the Hengill mountains. He asked the king to teach him how to defeat the troll and the king received his request favourably. He advised him to make his attack on Jóra at dawn on Whit Sunday, for, he said: "There is no being so evil nor troll so wild that it is not sleeping then. Remember to attack Jóra while she sleeps; she will be sleeping on her front. Here is an axe I shall give you," said the king, handing him a silver-inlaid axe. "Strike between the troll's shoulders. Jóra will wake up when she feels the pain, turn over and say: "Hands fast to the haft." Then you shall say: "Off with the axe." Both sayings shall have magical power and Jóra will tumble down to the lake near her cave, with the axe-blade between her shoulders. And the axe-blade will be washed up in a river, which will be known as the Axe River. And the Icelanders will subsequently locate their parliament there."

Thus spoke the king and the man thanked him for his advice and for the axe. He then went to Iceland and did exactly as the king had advised him and slew Jóra. The king's prophecy came true and the axe-blade was washed up in the river known since then as Öxará (Axe River), where the Icelanders chose to found their parliament at Þingvellir.

52. The Dance at Hruni

Between the two great rivers of Þjórsá and Hvítá is the district known as Hreppar: Gnúpverjahreppur to the east, Hrunamannahreppur to the west. Many visitors pass through this region, which boasts a number of interesting and picturesque sites, including Gullfoss (Golden Falls), Iceland's single most-visited tourist attraction, a splendid cascade at the edge of the central highlands. Most visitors to Gullfoss also stop at the Geysir geothermal area, which lies on the same route through Grímsnes and Biskupstungur. An alternative route to Gullfoss lies farther east, through Skeið and Hrunamannahreppur, crossing the Hvítá river at a narrow gorge named Brúarhlöð.

In Hrunamannahreppur there is a village called Flúðir, which has grown up around an area of hot springs, and now offers various facilities for visitors, including a hotel, campsite and restaurants. Close to the village of Flúðir is Hruni, which was once an important manor. From the late 12th century and into the 13th, Þorvaldur Gissurarson, a magnate of the Haukadalur clan, was pastor at Hruni. In 1224 he was one of those who founded a monastery on the island of Viðey, off the coast of Reykjavík; in his later years he was canon of the monastery. His son (priests were not required to be celibate in those days) was Gissur Þorvaldsson, who played an important role in Icelandic affairs in the 13th century and is the only earl in Icelandic history.

Many remarkable pastors have served the parish of Hruni over the centuries, including Jón Héðinsson, who was also steward at the nearby episcopal seat of Skálholt. At the height of the Reformation in

1539, when foreign bishops were attempting to force the new Lutheran order upon the Icelandic church, the Rev. Jón raised a posse to kill the Danish governor's henchman, Didrik von Minden, who had been pillaging monasteries and harassing monks.

Another pastor who served at Hruni is not known by name, though he is the subject of a well-known folk tale. Long ago, the church at Hruni stood on a hilltop above the farmhouse. The folk tale tells of how the church site came to be moved down to the lowlands near the farm:

There was once a pastor at Hruni who loved revels and entertainments. It was the custom of this pastor, when people came to church to attend Mass on Christmas Night, not to have any religious service during the early part of the night, as was usual, but instead to hold an entertainment for the parishioners, with dancing, drinking, games and other unseemly behaviour far into the night. The pastor's mother, whose name was Una, was with him at Hruni. She strongly disapproved of her son's behaviour and she often expressed her dissatisfaction to him. But he paid no attention and continued in the same way for many years.

One Christmas Night, the pastor remained longer at this dance in the church than was usual for him. His mother, who had the second sight and prophetic powers, went over to the church and asked her son to leave the dance and go to Mass. He protested that there was plenty of time and said: "One more turn, Mother, one more turn," and the dance went on. Una walked out of the church and into the farmhouse, but she was not happy and she returned a second and a third time to ask her son to think of God and give up the dance, before things went awry. He replied as before: "One more turn, Mother, one more turn," and the dance went on. But when Una walked down the aisle for the third time, she heard the following:

Hruni rings out in cheer,
the crowds draw near;
the dance will fill the air
remembered forever;
Una still is there
and Una still is there.

When Una came out of the church, she saw a man standing outside. She did not know him but did not like the look of him. She was sure that this man had spoken the verse. She was taken aback and saw that things had indeed gone awry, for it was the Devil himself.

She took her son's horse and rode as fast as she could to the pastor of the next parish. She told him the whole story and asked him to come and rescue her son, if possible, from the danger he was in. The pastor agreed at once, gathered together a large group from the congregation of his church and returned to Hruni with Una. But they were too late. When they arrived at Hruni, the church, the pastor and all his flock had vanished down into the bowels of the earth, and only howls and screams could be heard.

A new church was built below the hill after this and since then all the churches of Hruni have stood in the new location. But up on the hill there are still traces of a building that once stood there. The story says that after these terrifying events, there was never again dancing at Hruni on Christmas Night.

53. Bergþór the Giant of Bláfell

The Geysir geothermal area is one of Iceland's most popular and extraordinary tourist destinations. To reach Geysir, those heading east on the Ring Road should turn left by Mt. Ingólfsfjall, passing over the Sog river and through the Grímsnes and Biskupstungur districts. The huge spouting hot spring Geysir, which gave its name to geysers all over the world, used to spout to a height of 40–60 m. Geysir was dormant for much of the 20th century but was revived by two powerful earthquakes in 2000 and now spouts at irregular intervals. Nearby Strokkur (Butter Churn), however, is highly active, spouting every five or six minutes to a height of 20–30 m. In addition to these springs, the Geysir area abounds in hot pools and bubbling water and mud springs, including Litli Geysir (Little Geysir), Blesi and Smiður.

Geysir was the site of a sports college from 1927 until 1971, while today it has a hotel and restaurant, along with other tourist facilities.

Geysir is part of the estate of Haukadalur, which was an important manor in the days of the Old Commonwealth (930–1262). In the 11th century, a school was established at Haukadalur by Teitur Ísleifsson, founder of the Haukadalur clan, one of the most influential clans in medieval Iceland. Alumni of the Haukadalur school included the 12th-century scholar Ari Þorgilsson the Wise, Iceland's first historian.

In later centuries, the estate of Haukadalur suffered erosion and was ultimately abandoned. In 1938 Kristian Kirk from Denmark purchased the estate and began reforestation and other land reclamation.

On his death in 1940 the land passed to the Iceland Forestry Service, and afforestation has continued. Haukadalur now boasts mature and picturesque woods, and a monument to Kristian Kirk now stands there.

There has long been a church at Haukadalur. The present church building, which dates from 1842, was renovated by Kristian Kirk in 1940. The church has various old and interesting possessions, including an ancient door ring. North of the church is an oval hillock known as Bergþórsleiði (Bergþór's Grave), a name that recalls an old folk tale:

There was a man named Bergþór who lived in a cave in Mt. Bláfell. His wife was named Hrefna. Bergþór's father was named Þórólfur and he lived at Þórólfsfell, otherwise known as Kálfstindar. His mother was called Hlaðgerður and she lived at Hlöðufell. The country was heathen when this story happened. It was in the days of the troll-wife Hít, after whom the Hítardalur valley in west Iceland is named. Bergþór attended a gathering she held for all the trolls in the country at the Hundahellir cave in Hítardalur. After dinner, Hít arranged entertainment and invited the trolls to compete to find out who was the strongest. Bergþór was the strongest of them all.

Bergþór did no harm to men if they left him alone, but he was deemed to have prophetic powers and supernatural skills. After Iceland was converted to Christianity, his wife Hrefna was not happy at Bláfell, for they could see over the Christian community from there. She disliked this so much that she wanted to move north of the Hvítá river. Bergþór said it was of no importance and declared that he would stay in his cave. This did not change Hrefna's mind. She moved north of the river and built herself a house beneath a mountainside, which is known as Hrefnubúðir (Hrefna's Camp), north of the Hvítárvatn lake. After this, Bergþór and she met only when both went fishing for trout in the lake.

Bergþór often went down to Eyrarbakki on the south coast to buy flour, generally in winter when the lakes were frozen over; he usually brought back two barrels of flour. Once he was carrying his burden home and when he reached the homefield at Bergstaðir in Biskupstungur, he met the farmer and asked him for a drink. He said he would wait while the farmer brought it. He put his burden down by a rock and knocked a hole in the rock with the point of his stick. The farmer brought the drink and offered it to Bergþór. When Bergþór had drunk, he thanked the farmer and told him that he should keep his whey in the hollow he had made. He said that the whey would not be diluted by water, nor would it freeze, but that the farmer would lose heavily if he did not wish to use it. Then he bade farewell.

Once, in his old age, Bergþór met with the farmer of Haukadalur. He said he wished to choose a burial place for himself, where the sound of bells and the babbling of the river could be heard, and he asked the farmer to bring him to Haukadalur after his death. For this favour, the farmer could have what he kept in a cauldron by his bed. The farmer would know that Bergþór was dead when his walking stick appeared by the door of the farmhouse at Haukadalur.

One morning, a long time after this, when people arrived at Haukadalur, they noticed a huge stick standing by the farmhouse door. The farmer saw that it was Bergþór of Bláfell's stick and said little about it. He had a coffin built at once and set off for Bláfell with a small party of men. Nothing is reported of their journey until they reached Bergþór's Cave. They found Bergþór dead in his bed and they laid him in the coffin; they found him strangely light for his size.

Then the farmer saw a large cauldron by the bed and looked to see what was in it. All he saw was leaves, so he concluded that Bergþór had tricked him and did not take the cauldron with him. But one member of the party filled his gloves with the leaves. They carried Bergþór's body out of the cave and down from the mountain. When they arrived at the bottom, the man looked in his gloves and they were full of money. Then the farmer and his men went back, intending to fetch the cauldron, but they could not find the cave, however hard they looked, and it has never been found again. They had to abandon the search and returned home to Haukadalur.

The farmer had Bergþór interred north of the churchyard and the place has been known since then as Bergþórsleiði (Bergþór's Grave). The ring from Bergþór's walking stick is said to be the ring of the church door at Haukadalur. This is the end of the story of Bergþór, the giant of Bláfell.

54. Crossing the Falls at Gullfoss

Gullfoss, in the Hvítá river on the edge of the central highlands, is one of Iceland's most renowned and spectacular waterfalls. A natural formation of remarkable beauty, Gullfoss is the most-visited tourist attraction in Iceland. The waterfall is about 32 m high, falling in two cascades down into an impressive gorge up to 70 m deep. About 2.5 km in length, the gorge has been formed over the past 10,000 years, since the end of the last Ice Age, by the erosive action of the river. The gorge grows by about 25 cm in length each year, while the waterfall gradually progresses farther up the river. There is considerable vegetation at various points in the gorge, especially in a hollow called Pjaxi to the west of the gorge, where birch, grass and wildflowers flourish.

The name Gullfoss (Golden Falls) is believed to be inspired by the refraction of sunlight in the spray of the falls, which often forms a multiple rainbow. But legend also attributes the name to a hoard of gold and other valuables once flung into the waterfall by a wealthy farmer in the neighbourhood.

Gullfoss has been a major tourist attraction since travellers first began to visit Iceland. Tours to Gullfoss from Reykjavík were organised for tourists as long ago as the late 19th century. In those days, and long after, most of the visitors travelled on horseback and some on foot. When motor vehicles and roads arrived, the number of visitors rose dramatically. Official visitors and foreign potentates are also invariably taken to see Gullfoss. Some years ago, a restaurant operated there but this was later removed, with the aim of preserving the falls in their original, natural state. This has been achieved with remarkable success, in view of the number of people who visit the waterfall each summer.

Foreign investors soon saw potential for profit in the Golden Falls. In 1905, for instance, a wealthy Englishman approached Tómas, the farmer at Brattholt on whose property the falls were located, and offered him 50,000 crowns in gold for the waterfall. Tómas refused, saying that he would never sell his best friend. But some years later a foreign cartel gained control of the falls under a 150-year lease; they planned to harness the energy of the falls to generate electricity for industrial applications.

Sigríður, the daughter of Tómas of Brattholt, inherited the farm from her parents. She was always opposed to all plans for a power plant; she refused to accept the payments on the lease and took legal action to have the contract annulled. The legal proceedings went on for many years, costing Sigríður dearly in time and money, without achieving the desired result. But Sigríður won in the end, when the foreign company defaulted on its payments and the lease agreement was deemed void; after this the waterfall came into the possession of the Icelandic state.

Sigríður has been called Iceland's first conservationist, who campaigned for the conservation of one of Iceland's greatest treasures. She died in 1957 at the age of 85 and is buried in the churchyard at Haukadalur. She is commemorated by a plaque at the waterfall, by sculptor Ríkarð Jónsson.

Hvítá ("White River", a reference to the opaque waters of this glacier-fed torrent) is a large, fast-flowing river, and difficult to cross, although there are several fords which were used before the river was bridged. Upstream from Gullfoss the river plunges, white-foaming and wild, over rapids, before spreading out just above the waterfall. This does not seem a promising place to cross the river, but it has been done, according to at least one old tale:

In the late 17th century a farmer's son was growing up at Brattholt, west of the Hvítá river. On the other side of the river at that time, the daughter of the farmer and his wife at Hamarsholt was growing up, and the two were of very similar age. In the summer both looked after the sheep, herding the ewes to pasture on either side of the Hvítá, above Gullfoss. Soon they started calling to each other across the river and in time they became friends, though they had never met.

As the years passed their relationship developed, until each felt great affection for and attraction to the other. Eventually, when the young people were almost grown up, the boy called out an avowal of love across the river to the girl and asked her to be his wife. The girl received his proposal favourably, perhaps more in jest than in earnest, and said that she would marry him if he crossed the river to her. The lad did not hesitate but set off into the fast-flowing river just above the waterfall's edge. The river bottom was stony and the river much deeper in some places than others, so he had to tread with great care. It took a long time but he succeeded in crossing the river. On the other side the girl waited, torn between hope and fear, probably regretting that she had urged her friend to risk his life by wading across the river there. And so she gave him a warm welcome when he climbed out of the fast-flowing waters of the icy torrent. She kept her promise and that is the end of their story.

The two young people who declared their love across the Hvítá river more than three centuries ago were Þórður Guðbrandsson and Guðrún Þóroddsdóttir, who were married in 1690 and lived for many years at Fjall in the Skeið district. They had children and many generations of descendants.

55. The Holy Church at Engilsvík

Selvogur lies at the far western end of the southern lowlands, on Iceland's south coast. Today this is not regarded as a desirable place to live, as there are no harbour facilities, and sand drift and erosion have largely destroyed the vegetation. But in former times it was a different story; the farms yielded plenty of hay and had excellent pastures and some woods. The inhabitants also rowed out to fish off the coast, where fish stocks were abundant. In the west of the district is Hlíðarvatn lake, where the farmers fished for trout and gathered down from an eider colony. Almost all the farms in the district have now been abandoned, with the exception of Vogsósar.

The majority of the farms in Selvogur were laid waste by erosion over the past few centuries; this appears to have begun suddenly in the 17th century, causing massive damage in a matter of decades. At the manor of Strönd, for instance, there are said to have been seven or eight farms in the past; they were gradually deserted during the 17th century, until Strönd itself was abandoned in 1696. But the church survived, for the patch of land where it stood remained undamaged. In the 18th and 19th centuries it was often suggested that Strandarkirkja (Strönd Church) should be moved to Vogsósar, where the pastor lived. Bishops, deans and governors were in favour of this, as they felt it was not right to leave this sacred building out on the barren sands. But the Selvogur people opposed the idea; they felt that the church would lose its sanctity, and ultimately it was left where it was. According to tradition, the church was built on a sanctified spot and it should be allowed to remain there.

And Strönd Church still stands there, surrounded by a barren, uninhabited landscape. The Selvogur people still believe in its holiness, as do many others. The church is well known all over Iceland; people who find themselves in peril or in some kind of adversity, offer up prayers for help and promise some votive gift or contribution to the Strönd Church. It is commonly believed that such prayers are often answered.

Adjacent to the church is a sculpture, Landsýn *(View of Land) by Gunnfríður Jónsdóttir, which symbolises the story of how the church of Strönd came to be built:*

It was in the days of Bishop Árni Þorláksson of Skálholt that this story happened [i.e. the 13th century]. The bishop sent men to Norway to fetch timber to build a church. Their journey went well, until they were on their way home and found themselves in foul weather and lost their way at sea. They drifted for a long time, until finally they ran short of supplies and water, and it seemed that only death awaited them. They were strong young men, who foresaw this sad fate and had no idea what to do. When there seemed to be no hope for them, the captain called the crew together and told them to gather on deck and pray to reach land safely. They should promise to build a church from the cargo of the vessel, if they were so fortunate as to be saved. The crew were willing to do this and began to pray fervently.

Before long, the storm died down and they saw land at Selvogur. As they approached the shore, however, it seemed to them that they had no hope of landing due to the breakers and surf, and they prepared to sail away. But at that moment they saw a figure clad in white on the rocks by the shore; it held a shining cross and beckoned to them to approach. They did so, and landed safe and sound. Then they went ashore and looked around for the white figure who had guided them in but could not see it. They had come ashore in a little cove, which they named Engilsvík (Angel Cove), and it is known by that name still.

The crew did as they had promised in their prayers. They

went to Skálholt and told Bishop Árni their story, and he permitted them to use the timber they had brought from Norway to build a church at the place where they had come ashore. The church of the Selvogur people has stood there ever since, although the district has gradually become uninhabited.

Strönd Church appears to have had a special reputation from early times. Calling upon Strönd Church with prayers at times of sorrow, danger or illness proved successful, and the church accumulated considerable assets in money and goods. The oldest and most valuable item owned by the church is a 14th-century chalice of pure gold. In olden times, most gifts were in kind, for example the right to use timber from woods in Norway. But in modern times most gifts are of money, and people donate votive gifts to this church today as much as ever.

Thus Strönd Church is the wealthiest of all Icelandic churches, and has often loaned money to other parishes for construction of their churches. Many people who visit the south coast call in at Strönd Church for Sunday Mass, while others make a sort of pilgrimage to this place, which has had such a special reputation down through the centuries.

56. The Wizard Pastor of Vogsósar

The formerly flourishing region of Selvogur had suffered some damage due to sand drift and erosion by the time the Rev. Jón Westmann was appointed to serve the parish there. He was at Vogsósar from 1829 until 1842, when he was appointed to a benefice in Kjalarnes in the west. But he came to regret his rash decision to leave Selvogur and the excellent estate of Vogsósar, which had good pastures and plenty of hay, as well as various other valuable resources: trout fishing, an eider colony which provided costly down, seals which were caught for their meat and skins, dulse (a nourishing form of seaweed) and driftwood. Some time after leaving Selvogur, the Rev. Jón was heard to chant:

From Selvogur I miss
my sheep and my ewes,
trout and seals for the taking
but most sorely my trees.

Vogsósar, to the east of Hlíðarvatn lake, is located rather a long way from the other farms in the region, but close to the parish church of Strönd (see p. 199). Many renowned clergymen served the parish, until it was abolished in 1908. The most famous of them was certainly the Rev. Eiríkur Magnússon, who served at Selvogur from 1677 until his death in 1738. He was said to have great magical powers: he had been a pupil of the Rev. Jón Daðason of Arnarbæli, who was famed for his wizardry. The Rev. Eiríkur used his supernatural skills mainly to play harmless pranks, and never did any harm by his spells:

The Rev. Eiríkur started to perform magic at an early age, and he learned a great deal from an old book that he and his schoolmates got hold of when they were studying at the Skálholt School. This book, *Gráskinna* (Greyskin) (see p. 79), lay for a long time on a table in the schoolhouse at Skálholt. When Eiríkur became pastor at Vogsósar, he soon gained a reputation for supernatural and magical powers. News of this spread, until it finally reached the ears of the bishop, who was gravely displeased and summoned the pastor of Vogsósar to see him. The bishop brought out *Gráskinna* and asked the Rev. Eiríkur whether he knew what was in the book. Eiríkur took the book, leafed through it for a while and said: "I don't know one letter of this." The bishop had him swear an oath that he was telling the truth, and then allowed him to return home. Some time later Eiríkur told his friends that he knew every letter of the book but one, though he asked them to ensure that the bishop did not hear of this.

Many young men came to the Rev. Eiríkur and asked to be taught magic. He tested them in various ways and took as apprentices those he found promising. Once a young lad came to him and asked to be instructed. "Stay with me until Sunday and come to Krýsuvík with me. Then I'll tell you whether I will accept you as a pupil," the Rev. Eiríkur told him. On the following Sunday they set off and rode along the sands. Then the Rev. Eiríkur halted and said to the lad: "I've left my handbook at home. It's under my pillow. Go and fetch it for me but don't open it on the way." The boy turned back, fetched the book and rode out along the sands. But he could not resist opening the book and starting to read. Instantly, he was surrounded by demons asking: "What shall I do? What shall I do?" The lad was resourceful, however, and said: "Plait the sands into a rope." The demons sat down on the sand and began to plait a rope, which was not possible, of course. The lad soon caught up with the pastor, who took the book and said: "You have opened this." The boy denied it. They continued on their way and the pastor celebrated Mass at Krýsuvík. On the way home, they came to the sands, where the demons were busily at work. Then the pastor said: "I knew you had opened the book, dear boy, although you denied it. But you reacted cleverly and it would be worth teaching you something." This lad then entered the Rev. Eiríkur's school.

Another lad who asked for instruction was sent by the Rev. Eiríkur out to Strönd Church to fetch a pair of gloves he had left there. The lad went and found the gloves, but when he went to pick them up, all the fingers moved. He was afraid, and returned to the pastor and told him what had happened. Rev. Eiríkur then said: "Go home, dear boy; I cannot teach you anything."

Once a young man on his way to the fishing station called at Vogsósar and stayed the night. In the evening this man was very sad and sorrowful, so the Rev. Eiríkur took him aside and asked what was the matter. The man was reluctant to tell him but finally agreed. He said that his sweetheart had broken off with him before he left on his journey. He asked the pastor for help but Eiríkur was unwilling and said it was a difficult matter.

In the evening the pastor had one man go to sleep in each bed, while he stayed awake far into the night. There was a knock at the door and the pastor answered it. A girl was there, rather poorly dressed and wet through, for it was raining heavily. She greeted the pastor and asked for shelter, as she was near perished with cold. He invited her in and asked how she came to be on the road. She said that while she was getting ready for bed, she had gone out to check whether the laundry had been taken in, as it was starting to rain. She had lost her way in the dark and did not know where she was until she found herself at the farmhouse door at Vogsósar. The Rev. Eiríkur told her that it would be difficult to put her up overnight, as all the beds were occupied. So there was no room for her, unless she was prepared to lie down with that man over there – and he pointed out the distressed traveller, who lay stock-still in his bed. She said she would rather do that than die of cold. Then she lay in the bed next to the guest, and he recognised his former sweetheart and she him. She stayed there with him that night and they got on well. After that they were married and lived happily ever after.

57. The Merman Laughed

Vogar is a thriving community on Faxaflói bay, with about 500 inhabitants. This was once the manor of Stóru-Vogar, with many small farms around it where people made their living by a combination of animal husbandry and fishing. In the late 19th century Vogar began to grow into a village, especially after it became a licensed trading port in 1893. South of Vogar is Vogastapi, with steep cliffs down to the sea. Below it were rich fishing grounds in former times, known as Gullkista (Treasure Chest). Ghosts have long been reputed to haunt Vogastapi, and in past centuries many people lost their way there and fell to their deaths from the cliffs or died of exposure. Even today rumours are heard of hauntings; motorists on the main road have been known to see a man walking with his head under his arm. The Stapi Ghost sometimes even joins people in their cars, if they are travelling alone in dark conditions.

The people of the district have long made their living from the sea and they have a reputation for being determined fishermen, who were not easily discouraged. Once the farmer of Vogar caught a merman on his hook, as the folk tale tells:

In the Suðurnes region there is a hamlet named Vogar, or Kvíguvogar as it is called in the *Book of Settlements*. Once a farmer lived there who was a keen fisherman, for the place has some of the best fishing in all south Iceland. One day the farmer rowed out as usual and nothing is told of the fish he caught. But he hooked something heavy and when he had pulled it up by the boat, he saw that it was of human shape and hauled it aboard. The farmer discovered that the man was alive and he asked him where he was from. The man said he was a merman from the bottom of the sea. He said he had been caught by the farmer's hook when he was fixing his mother's kitchen chimney. He asked the farmer to let him go down again, but the farmer said that was not possible and that the merman would have to stay with him. After that the merman would not speak to him.

A short while later the farmer went ashore, taking the merman with him. When he had beached his vessel, his dog came down to him and jumped up to greet him. The farmer was angry and struck the dog a blow. Then the merman laughed for the first time. The farmer went on up the home-field and tripped over a tussock and cursed it. Then the merman laughed a second time. The farmer went on to the farm-house. His wife came out and greeted him affectionately and he responded warmly to her welcome. Then the merman laughed a third time.

The farmer said to the merman: "You have laughed three times and I am curious to know why you laughed." "I won't tell you," said the merman, "unless you take me back to the place where you caught me." The farmer agreed. Then the merman said: "I laughed for the first time when you struck your dog, for he came to greet you with affection. I laughed again when you tripped over the tussock and cursed it, for it is full of gold. And I laughed for the third time when you happily received the cant of your wife, for she deceives you and is unfaithful. Now you must fulfil your promise to me and return me to the fishing grounds where you caught me."

The farmer said: "Two of the things you said – the affection of my dog and the faithfulness of my wife – cannot be tested at present, but I shall test the truth of what you say about gold being hidden in the tussock. If this is so, it is more likely that the other things are true too, and I shall fulfil my promise."

Then the farmer went and dug up the tussock. He found a hoard of money there, as the merman had said. Then he launched his vessel and returned the merman to the same fishing grounds where he had caught him. But before the farmer released him, the merman said: "You have acted well, farmer, in returning me to my mother, and I shall repay you, if you know how to make use of what you receive. Farewell, farmer." Then the farmer let him down into the depths and no more is said of the merman. But the merman's laughter is commemorated by a rhyme:

I remember his laughter,
the merman's, so loud;
sweet his treasure after
landwards he rowed;
he kissed the fair maid
though false she was found,
but the great hero flayed
his poor blameless hound.

Shortly after this, the farmer was told that seven cows, sea-grey in colour, were at the edge of the homefield by the sea. He responded quickly, grabbing a staff as he went. He went to where the cows were; they were restless and uneasy. He noticed that each cow had a bladder over her mouth, and he realised that he would lose the cows unless he could burst the bladders. He struck at the face of one cow and managed to catch her but all the others escaped into the sea. Now the farmer concluded that the merman had sent him the cows in thanks for releasing him. The cow he caught proved to be the most excellent beast known in Iceland. Cattle descended from her were dispersed all over Iceland, all grey in colour, and known as the "sea-cow breed". The farmer became a wealthy man, and changed the name of Vogar (Bays) to Kvíguvogar (Heifer Bays), after the cows that had come ashore there.

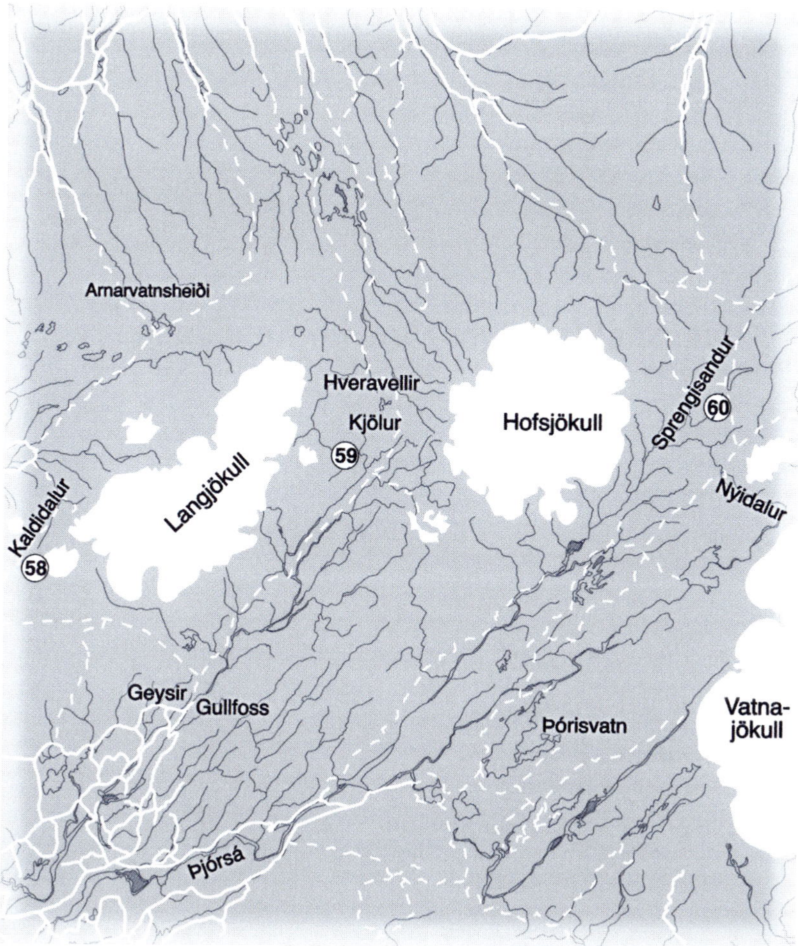

Arnarvatnsheiði
Hveravellir
Kjölur
59
Hofsjökull
Sprengisandur
60
Langjökull
Kaldidalur
58
Nýidalur
Geysir
Gullfoss
Þórisvatn
Vatna-
jökull
Þjórsá

HIGHLANDS

58. Skúli's Flight through Kaldidalur

The Kaldidalur road is the mountain route between Árnessýsla in the south and Borgarfjörður in the west via Kaldidalur (Cold Valley), an alternative to the long route around the west coast. This route was travelled on foot and on horseback over the centuries, long before Iceland had any roads. In 1830 a path was cleared on the Kaldidalur route and a century later a road was built for motor vehicles. In 1930, when thousands of Icelanders gathered at Þingvellir to celebrate the millennium of the Althing (parliament), many travellers from the north and west drove over Kaldidalur – at this time the west-coast road had not been completed.

Starting from the tourist information centre at Þingvellir, travellers heading for Kaldidalur should drive towards Bolabás and alongside Ármannsfell. Before long, the road reaches a broad plain, Hofmannaflöt, between Ármannsfell and Mjóafell; ahead lies a hill named Meyjarsæti (Maiden's Seat). Old tales tell that all Iceland's trolls used to gather to play games at Hofmannaflöt while spectators watched from Meyjarsæti.

The road lies through a pass on the south side of Meyjarsæti and along by Sandkluftavatn lake, where there are extensive sands and sometimes sandstorms. It then passes through Ormavellir and up the steep and rocky Tröllaháls (Trolls' Ridge), followed by Víðiker (Willow Hollow) and Biskupsbrekka (Bishop's Slope). To the right is a splendid view of Mt. Skjaldbreið and of Hlöðufell farther east. Biskupsbrekka is named after Bishop Jón Vídalin. On his way to the west in 1720, he suddenly fell ill and died in a mountain shack here.

The bishop had apparently been apprehensive about the journey, as before setting off he spoke this verse:

Lord in Thy hall on high
help my faith be bold;
the hour of night is nigh,
fear gnaws me in the Valley of Cold.

Before long, the road passes Hallbjarnarvörður (Hallbjörn's Cairns), named after a certain Hallbjörn Oddsson: he married Hallgerður, the daughter of Oddur of Tunga, and they spent the winter after their marriage at Breiðabólsstaður in the Reykholt valley. There was said to be little affection between them. In the spring Hallbjörn wanted to return to his home district in the south but Hallgerður refused to go with him. Hallbjörn was angry, so he grabbed her thick hair, wound it around his hand and chopped off her head with his sword. After this he fled into Kaldidalur, pursued by Hallgerður's kinsman Snæbjörn, who fought Hallbjörn and killed him. The cairns were built in memory of those who died in the battle.

From Hallbjarnarvörður the road passes through Brunnar, a marsh with two small lakes. Ahead lies the hill Fanntófell and to the right Hrúðurkarlar and Björnsfell. The Þórisjökull glacier is also clearly visible.

The route soon passes Beinakerling (Bone Woman), a large and well-built cairn, which marks the halfway point of the journey from Þingvellir to Húsafell in Borgarfjörður. In former times mountain travellers often made up verses, generally obscene in nature, and these were known as beinakerlingarvísur (Bone-woman Verses). This verse is supposed to be spoken by the great cairn itself:

The finest lads descend in swarms
upon me as if driven mad.
In Cold Valley with open arms
alone I lie and wait, my lad.

The road passes along Langihryggur, reaching 727 m above sea level. To the west is Sléttalág, part of a huge fissure in the earth's surface.

The road has now reached the actual valley of Kaldidalur, which lies between the Ok and Langjökull glaciers. Between Þórisjökull and Geitlandsjökull is the Þórisdalur valley; according to the Saga of Grettir, the hero Grettir Ásmundarson dwelt there for a time with a giant named Þórir. At the mouth of the valley is Mt. Prestahnjúkur, which is rich in perlite, a glassy form of rhyolite.

Descending from Langihryggur, the road turns to the northeast through rocky territory east of the Geitá river, then follows the river down to the lowlands at Húsafell. Part of this rocky plain west of Langihryggur is known as Skúlaskeið (Skúli's Run), after a certain Skúli:

The folk tale of Skúli says that he had committed some serious offence and been condemned to death at the Althing (parliament), which also served as a high court. The sentence was to be carried out at the parliamentary site. But at the last moment Skúli managed to evade his guards, mount his steed Sörli and flee. He was pursued by a large number of people but he got away from them, because his horse was so swift-footed. He rode northwards via Hofmannaflöt, Tröllaháls, Víðiker, Hallbjarnarvörður and then Kaldidalur, where he stopped briefly and dismounted. His pursuers were still some distance behind him, as they could not keep up with Sörli. When Skúli saw them approach, he poured a few drops of drink from his canteen and called out to them that this was their reward for sending him such a large escort. Then he remounted and galloped off along one of the worst and stoniest routes in Iceland (still known today as Skúlaskeið or "Skúli's Run"). Skúli escaped and reached his home but the horse fell down dead from exhaustion. To honour this excellent horse, which had saved his life, Skúli had the animal buried with ceremony and held a funeral wake.

59. *Ghosts are Abroad on Kjölur*

Ever since the *Age* of Settlement (9th–10th centuries), the Kjölur route has been an important link between north and south Iceland. By far the most direct route, the Kjölur trail leads straight across the uninhabited highlands between the Langjökull and Hofsjökull glaciers, a distance of only about 165 km.

In olden times the Kjölur route had many variants, but since the advent of the automobile, the route begins (at the southern end) west of the Hvítá river and Mt. Bláfell. Travellers may set off on to the rocky and barren plateau from the Gullfoss waterfall (see p. 196). To the left is the Langjökull glacier and to its south Hagafell hill and the Hagavatn lake. Farther north is a series of peaks, Jarlhettur, the highest of which are more than 1,000 m in height. Mt. Bláfell lies ahead, the highest mountain in the southwest, at 1,204 m. Folklore says that this was the home of Bergþór the Giant (see p. 192).

The route passes over the Bláfellsháls ridge, where passers-by often add a rock or two to a huge cairn. It is said that more than half a century ago, the men who built the road left their tattered gloves and boots behind when the work was finished, covering them with rocks. Then others who passed along the road added more rocks and so on, resulting in the massive cairn that stands today.

North of Mt. Bláfell is a view over the Hvítárvatn lake and the glaciers beyond. A bridge crosses the Hvítá river and the road continues northwards by the lake. It is well worth taking a short diversion down to Hvítárnes, an extensive area of marshland west of Tjarnheiði, the site of the oldest mountain lodge of the Iceland Touring Club, dating from 1930. Hvítárvatn lake is about 30 km^2 in area, and lies 419 m above sea level; on the waters of the lake drift ice floes, which have calved from the glaciers on the opposite side. North of the lake is Hrefnubúðir, where birch shrubs grow on the slopes at an altitude higher than almost anywhere else in the country. East of the mountain lodge are remnants of a farmhouse from the Saga Age. The place is reputed to be haunted and not all guests in the lodge manage to sleep soundly.

The road continues northwards, west of Fremri-Skúti and east of Innri-Skúti. To the left is the ice-capped Mt. Hrútfell. At Gránunes, a right turn leads to the Kerlingarfjöll mountains, where a ski school operates in summer below the peaks Loðmundur and Snækollur. The white expanses of the Hofsjökull glacier rise up to an altitude of 1,800 m, while ahead are the mountains of Kjölur: Kjalfell, Rjúpnafell and Dúfunefsfjall. South of Dúfunefsfjall, horse races were reputedly held long ago by Þórir dúfunef (Þórir Pigeon-beak) and a certain Örn. Þórir won the race and Örn was so dejected that he disappeared on the mountain that now bears his name, Arnarfell (Örn's Hill).

Beyond Beinahóll (Bone Hill) is Hveravellir, a geothermal area in the middle of the highlands, with a mountain lodge, swimming pool, weather observation station, etc. Nearby are the remnants of a shack, where Iceland's most famous outlaw, Eyvindur Jónsson, known as Mountain-Eyvindur (Fjalla Eyvindur), lived with his lover Halla in the 18th century (see p. 219).

Northeast of Kjalfell, a short walk in the lava field leads to Beinahóll (Bone Hill), where Bjarni Halldórsson and his brother Einar, the Reynistaður brothers, died of exposure together with several companions in the autumn of 1780, along with many sheep and horses. No one survived to tell exactly what happened and there was much speculation about how the brothers had met their end. They had travelled south to buy sheep and set off in late autumn to cross Kjölur to the north, but were caught in a blizzard and died at Kjalhraun.

One of the party, Jón Austmann, is supposed to have tried

to reach the nearest habitation to the north. He is believed to have died at Blöndugil. One of his hands was later found there and identified by its glove.

When the Reynistaður brothers did not reach home as planned, there were fears that something had happened to them. Their sister Björg dreamed that Bjarni came to her and spoke this verse:

No one can ever find us
in our snow-driven tomb.
Three days instead beside the dead
Bjarni sat in gloom.

The following spring, a traveller on his way south across the highlands found their tent; he said he saw four bodies. When other people arrived at the place shortly afterwards, there were only two bodies and not those of the Reynistaður brothers. This led to outrage and to legal proceedings, as the inference was drawn that someone had robbed the bodies and hidden the remains of the brothers.

Björg dreamed again that her brother visited her and said:

In a rocky cleft we brothers lie huddled,
in a tent there before
we all rested together.

The case was never solved conclusively, and it was not until sixty-five years later that bones were discovered, which were believed to be those of the brothers. Bones of sheep and horses still turn up at Beinahóll today. In 1971 a memorial to the Reynistaður brothers was erected.

There are still rumours of ghosts walking in this place; it is said that when people camp there, a shadow sometimes falls on the tent as if someone is passing by, but no one can be seen.

The road continues north past Hveravellir and across Auðkúluheiði, between hills and lakes. Mt. Mælifellshnjúkur rises up from the plateau in the northeast, leading towards the green valleys of north Iceland.

60. Outlaws and Spirits on Sprengisandur

The Sprengisandur route is the longest road across the highlands between north and south Iceland, and it reaches the highest altitude of any of the highland roads. This route has been travelled since the earliest days of Iceland's history; in Njál's Saga it is called Gásasandur (Goose Sands), a reference to the pink-footed geese which breed in summer at Þjórsárver in the central uplands. The bishops of Skálholt generally travelled the Sprengisandur route when they visited their parishes in the east. On one such occasion, a man named Þórður was supposed to wait near Kiðagil for Bishop Oddur Einarsson, who was travelling from the south. The bishop was delayed and Þórður began to run short of food. He composed the following verse, which he carved in the ground before leaving:

I wait for the bishop, brought
by hunger to my knees.
Before heading for Oddur's court
I dined on mouldy cheese.

In the past, the Sprengisandur route began at Skriðufell in the Þjórsá valley, crossing the river by a ford at Sóleyjarhöfði, though some travellers set off from Galtalækur, crossing the Tungnaá river by ferry. The Sprengisandur route was about 240 km, from Skriðufell to Mýri in Bárðardalur. This long journey across the barren highlands was hard for both men and horses, not least due to the lack of grazing for the animals along the way. Relatively few people made this journey across the highlands and the Sprengisandur route is believed to have been entirely abandoned by about 1700.

Attempts were made to resume journeys in the late 18th century, and during the 19th century people occasionally travelled the Sprengisandur route. In 1835, the Rev. Tómas Sæmundsson, dean at Breiðabólsstaður in south Iceland, made the journey with an escort of men. The weather was bad and they lost their way. The Rev. Tómas went looking for shelter and came across a small patch of pasture for the horses, which has been called Tómasarhagi (Tómas's Pasture) ever since.

Ten years later, in 1845, an expedition set off from Bárðardalur in the north to explore the highlands, and discovered a grassy valley south of Tungnafell, which they named Nýi Jökuldalur (New Glacier Valley). In 1858 Konrad Maurer from Germany travelled across Sprengisandur, and in 1897 the Danish scientist Daniel Bruun made the journey, after which he urged that the route be marked by cairns.

In the 20th century increasing use was made of the route; in 1916, for instance, Sturla Jónsson walked from Bárðardalur to Gnúpverjahreppur in the south in three days, when the highlands were still entirely blanketed in snow. In 1925, L. H. Muller travelled the route but had bad weather and was nearly a week on the way. Þórður Flóventsson of Svartárkot in north Iceland made the most use of the Sprengisandur route before the advent of the motor car; he herded his sheep across the highlands, making "shoes" for them to protect their hooves from the sharp rocks.

The first journey across Sprengisandur by car was made in 1933 and after Hófsvað, a ford over the Tungnaá river, was discovered in 1949, motor travel began in earnest. Some time later, a pulley-operated car ferry was installed for transport across the river, and a bridge was finally built at Sigalda in 1968, when a hydroelectric power station was under construction.

Starting from the south, the Sprengisandur route now lies east of the Þjórsá river, across the Tungnaá river at Hraunyejar, north by Þórisvatn lake, across the Kaldakvísl river by a bridge, then via Þveralda, Hnötóttaalda, Skrokkalda and Kistualda to Nýidalur, south of Mt. Tungnafell, where an excellent mountain lodge is located. The route then leads on northward via Tómasarhagi, west of Fjórðungsalda, *through Kiðagilsdrög and Fossgilsmosi, and down into Bárðardalur. From the Sprengisandur road, the Gæsavötn road leads to the Dyngjufjöll mountains, and also to Eyjafjörður and Skagafjörður in the north.*

The Sprengisandur route has long had a reputation for mystery and danger, as witness Á Sprengisandi *(On Sprengisandur), a poem by Grímur Thomsen, which is still a favourite song with Icelanders today.*

Ride on, ride on, race across the black sand.
Round the mountain the sun is going down,
evil spirits are sporting in the dark land,
shadows falling on the glacier's crown.
Lord, pray lead my horse by your will,
for long is the stretch I must travel still.

Legend has it that outlaws and fugitives from justice lived a hand-to-mouth existence in the highlands, and there are some documented cases of this. The following is an excerpt from a report made by Einar Brynjólfsson from Stóri-Núpur, after he apprehended the outlaw Eyvindur Jónsson (Mountain-Eyvindur) and his wife Halla (see p. 214) on Sprengisandur in 1772:

"Soon we reached a small brook with a little grass on either side. The path led this way and we followed it until we spotted some shacks and nearby a few sheep. I loaded the handgun I had brought with me; my companions, however, were unarmed and they grasped their sticks and tent-poles. We led the advance and saw two people leaving the shack. When we made for them, one turned back towards us, first throwing down what he had been carrying. He approached us and greeted each of us. I asked his name, to which he replied: "My name is Jón." But when I refused to believe that this was his true name, he answered: "To tell the truth, my real name is Eyvindur Jónsson." The other person, who wore a coat of sheepskin, was his wife. She came to us also.

Both begged us fervently for life and mercy. We took both of them with us and left their hovel about half an hour before noon."

Folklore tells of a certain Starkaður from Stóruvellir in Bárðardalur in the north. His sweetheart lived in the south, at Stóri-Núpur or Þrándarholt. He set off across Sprengisandur to visit her but was caught in bad weather and died of exposure below a rock, which now bears his name, Starkaðarsteinn (Starkaður's Rock). The place itself is also named after him, Starkaðarver. At about the time of his death, his betrothed dreamed that Starkaður came to her and spoke the following verse:

Sorrows and harms for a woman's charms
men have often suffered.
Starkaður's bones under the stones
still lie undiscovered.

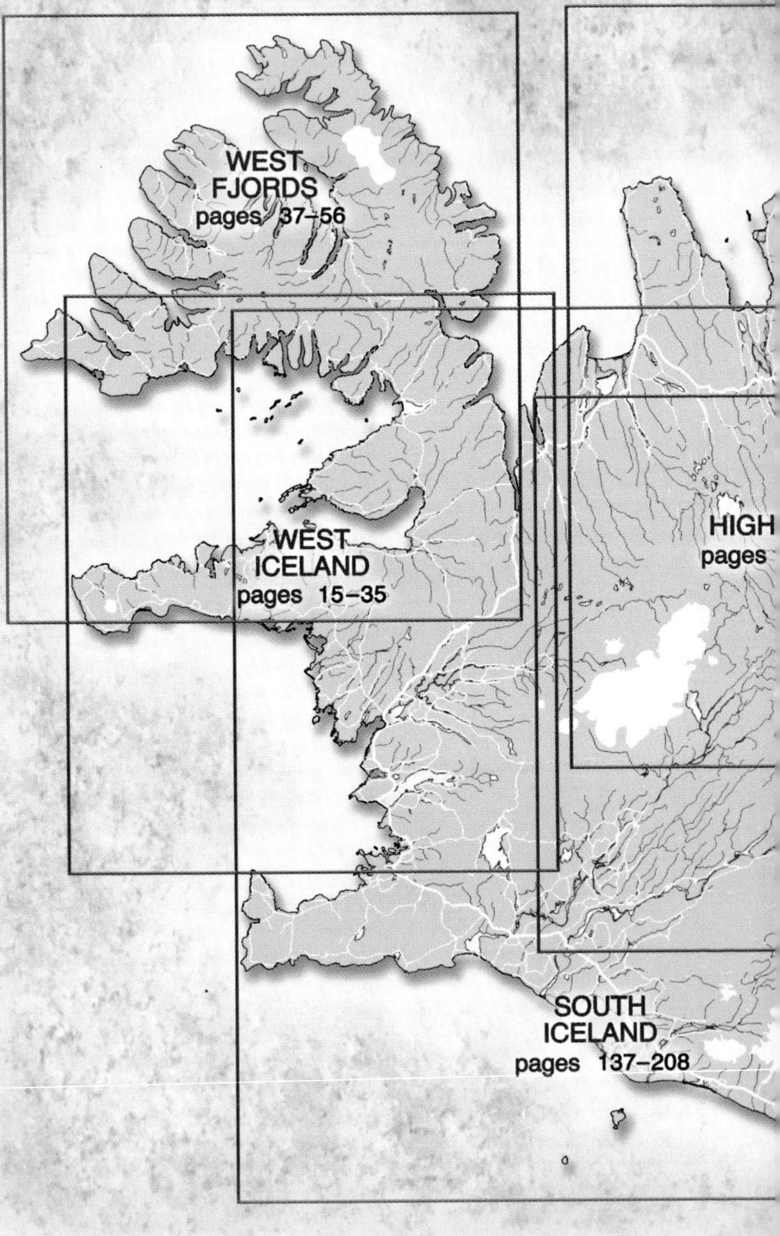
WEST
FJORDS
pages 37–56
WEST
ICELAND
pages 15–35
HIGH
pages
SOUTH
ICELAND
pages 137–208